FEAR INC.

VOLUME 2

MELINDA VALENTINE

LIMITLESS PUBLISHING, LLC

Fear Inc: Volume 2

Copyright © 2017 by Melinda Valentine.

All rights reserved.

First Print Edition: May 2017

Limitless Publishing, LLC

Kailua, HI 96734

www.limitlesspublishing.com

Formatting: Limitless Publishing

ISBN-13: 978-1-64034-102-9

DEDICATION

To my parents, Linda and Leslie.

Thank you for the endless supply of books as a child, for not grounding me every time you found me under the covers with a flashlight reading well past my bedtime, and most importantly, for encouraging me to always chase my dreams. This one is for you. I love you both.

ONE
TANK

PAXTON PULLED into the driveway of his simple, one-story ranch just as the sun was coming up over the horizon. He was exhausted from the all-night stakeout he'd just finished—his limbs were sore from sitting in his truck for so many hours. On the plus side, his client would be happy to know her husband had, in fact, worked late at his office before going to the small apartment he owned in the city for the rest of the night. This was the third and last night Paxton would have to follow the man around.

He unfolded his cramped body out of the driver's seat. Stretching his arms above his head, he could hear the joints pop and crack.

His left leg bothered him more than anything else. The bullet that shattered his knee had left him with a nasty scar and a slight limp, which was more pronounced in the colder weather. Even so, most people didn't notice it unless they were looking for it. It had, however, given him a one-way ticket to a desk job in the Bush Castle PD.

Paxton was not cut out to be a desk jockey. Leaving the BCPD had been one of the hardest decisions he'd ever had to make, but getting his private investigator's license seemed like the next best thing to being a cop. The downside, however, was working for a divorce attorney. All he seemed to do was follow around unfaithful spouses. That seriously put a wrench in the way he viewed relationships.

Now and again, however, he was able to prove a client wrong, like today. Those were good days.

He'd wished he could've proven his client wrong two years ago. He'd followed his "mark" around for three days. On the third day, Paxton had been surprised to find himself in his own neighborhood. An eerie feeling had taken root in his gut; he'd learned to always listen to that little voice, as nagging as it could sometimes be. It had served him well in his years on the police force. There he'd sat across from the house he'd shared with Gillian. He'd watched the man he was being paid to follow kiss his own fiancée hello.

Paxton could hardly believe his eyes. Through the lens of his camera, he watched the man pick her up and carry her into the house. Gillian squealed with delight.

What was he supposed to do? The woman he loved was in bed with another man. Not just *any* bed—his bed. *Their* bed. He'd felt as though his heart had been ripped out. She'd never giggled like that when he came home. Paxton knew it was over. In the process, his faith in love had been irrevocably damaged.

He pulled his duffel bag from the passenger seat, and movement from the corner of his eye caught his attention. Across the yard, a young woman carried boxes from the trunk of her car to the front porch. She was petite with long raven hair that shimmered in the sunlight.

Paxton had secretly watched her every day this week. On more than one occasion, he'd thought about offering help, but quickly changed his mind. He wasn't interested in getting involved with anyone, and having a one-night stand with a neighbor wasn't the smartest thing to do. He took one more look before heading up to his house.

He was excited about the future for the first time in a long time. This job was his final one for Schmidt & Frankel, attorneys at law. Starting Monday morning, he would be working for his longtime friend, Maxwell Fear. They had gone through the academy together years ago. Even after they both left the force, they stayed close.

A few months after things went to shit with Gillian, Max got himself tangled up with a woman named Sloane. The Russian mob wanted her dead after she witnessed her boss' murder. Paxton—along with Gutter Mouth, Mother, and Foster—helped keep her safe when Max wasn't able to.

Now, almost eighteen months later, Sloane would be running the office of the business Max built, Fear Incorporated. Since they still worried about the Petrov family, having her and their daughter, Mia, surrounded by ex-cops all day was a smart move.

Paxton entered his house and dropped his duffel on the floor by the door. His report to Schmidt & Frankel could wait until after a hot shower and a nap. He quickly sent them an email using his smartphone, informing the partners that Mr. Everhart was in fact being faithful to his wife. They could inform the woman without his full report. He'd send the details later.

He pulled his shirt over his head. Paxton tossed it into his laundry wicker basket. His jeans and socks followed after that. He turned the water on, brushing his teeth as he waited for it to heat up. He looked at himself in the mirror. His hair was starting to grow back in.

After his breakup, he'd shaved his head bald. Couple that with his height and tattoos, and it made him an intimating man. It helped keep people at arm's length. He rubbed his hand across his head, feeling the prickly hairs brush his palm. He needed to shave again.

Stepping into the shower, Paxton groaned the instant the hot spray washed over his sore muscles. He stood there letting the water beat on his shoulders and back, slowly easing some of the tension away. Turning off the now lukewarm water, he wrapped a towel around his waist.

He left the bathroom, a trail of water dripping behind him. He strode down the hallway to his bedroom. He checked his phone, relieved no one had contacted him.

His basketball shorts lay waiting for him at the foot of the bed. He pulled them on, cringing slightly as his knee popped. He rubbed the soreness out of habit, but it wouldn't do a damn thing to take the pain away. Not bothering with a shirt, Paxton headed back out to his living room. He plopped on the couch, turned on ESPN, and closed his eyes.

He was just beginning to relax when he was startled by a knock on the door. No one *ever* knocked on his door. Curious, he shoved off the worn couch. On the other side of the door was his raven-haired neighbor. *Interesting.*

Paxton opened the door. "Can I help you?"

"I hope so." She smiled warmly. "I'm your new neighbor, Cori."

He nodded. "Paxton."

"Well, I hate to impose, but my shed door seems to be stuck. I've tried to get it open every day this week to no avail. Would you mind helping me?"

Paxton wouldn't let one of his neighbors struggle with

anything if he could help; he often carried in Mrs. Thomas's groceries. She was in her seventies and her son rarely paid her a visit. Sometimes he would sit and talk with her for a little while. She had some wild stories of when she was younger. So of course, he'd try to help Cori too.

"Sure, let me grab some shoes." He turned and slipped on a pair of sneakers. After stepping outside, he motioned for her to go. "Lead the way."

The house had been sold three weeks ago, but he'd only begun to see the woman around this past week. He followed her around the house to where the shed was in the backyard.

She sure was a tiny thing...couldn't be taller than five-foot-two. Her ass swayed naturally with every step she took, and his gaze kept dropping to watch it. When she finally turned to face him in front of the shed, he noticed that she had a pert nose and pouty lips painted with some kind of shiny gloss. *Wonder if it's flavored...*He quickly shook that thought out of his head. He reminded himself —yet again—that he didn't do relationships and banging the cute little neighbor would be a *very* bad idea.

"This is it." She placed both hands on her slender hips, as if Paxton couldn't plainly see the shed in front of them. He smiled in spite of himself.

Her fingernails were painted a light pink. Did her toes match? Why he found that so intriguing was a mystery to him.

He stepped forward and grabbed ahold of the handle. He tugged once. Twice. The third time, Paxton braced his other hand on the shed wall before yanking hard. The structure let out a loud shriek before the door gave way. The force rattled things off their pegs inside.

Paxton frowned at the small shards of wood littering the ground. "This all looks dry rotted."

Cori rubbed the bridge of her nose. "Of *course* it is. Why wouldn't it be? Everything else is going wrong."

He stayed quiet, watching tears well up in her eyes. What was he supposed to say? The house had been vacant for almost a year. He'd never gone inside, but the kids who'd lived in the place before hadn't looked like they could take care of *themselves*, much less a whole house. Besides, he didn't know anything about this woman except she had a fine ass. Her woes weren't his problem. He decided to make his escape before she started seeking comfort in the wrong places.

"Anything else?" he asked.

She sniffled. "No, thank you for your help."

Without answering her, Paxton barreled back across the yard to his house. He couldn't take a woman in tears. Once inside, he kicked off his shoes and regained his position on the couch. Within moments, he was asleep.

TWO
CORI

THE MAN WAS A BEAST—HE was definitely more than a foot taller than her. He was also curt, rude, and sexy as hell. His extremely short dark hair, massive size, and tattoo-covered body only made him more intimidating. Cori's eyes weren't sure where they wanted to feast first. She briefly wondered what his beard would feel like against her tender skin.

She'd been unusually nervous knocking on his door. She'd known he'd taken the time to watch her move her things in—she could see him in the window and feel his eyes on her the entire time.

She'd thought that maybe he was interested in her, but judging by their first encounter, she'd clearly been mistaken.

Not that she needed to get involved with anyone, anyway. She'd moved to this sleepy town in West Virginia to get away from everything and focus on herself. As a psychiatrist, Cori knew the importance of mental health, and sometimes a person just needed to take a step back and take care of themselves. That's what she needed right now. After one of her patients, Rebecca Williams, killed herself, Cori decided to temporarily close her practice.

Her other patients hadn't been too pleased with the change, but she had to get away. Rebecca's husband was becoming a problem. He'd called her every hour for a week following his wife's death, and every call was the same: He blamed Cori. His beloved wife was dead because Cori couldn't fix her. But what Cori couldn't do was make Rebecca leave her abusive husband. Instead, the woman had taken her own life to get away from him.

Knowing it wasn't her fault and feeling it wasn't her fault were two totally different things. So here she was in a little town she'd never heard of, living next to a giant of a man in a house that needed more work than she'd thought, at least from the pictures she'd seen. Served her right for buying a house without visiting it first.

Nevertheless, Cori liked the house and it wasn't like she had anything better to do. Without her practice, she had all day, every day, to do whatever she wanted. Fixing up this old house was the perfect thing to keep her busy— in both body *and* mind.

She carefully entered the shed. Everything inside was covered in a layer of dust. Cobwebs hung from…well, just about everything. They made her shiver. She was not a fan of eight-legged creatures. Not at all. Unfortunately, she didn't think a can of bathroom cleaner was going to do the trick of getting rid of them in here. With the dry rot also being a problem, she decided it would be so much easier to just replace the shed altogether.

Decision made, she bounded back into the house to make a few calls. No matter what task she focused on, she couldn't stop herself from picturing Tall, Dark, and Grumpy. He was one hell of a male specimen. She wondered if he was just having a bad day or if he was always so charming. They were neighbors, after all. Weren't small towns supposed to have friendly neighbors? The kind that waved to you and had an overachiever as the head of the neighborhood watch?

Obviously she would need to cut down on her television time—it was skewing her expectations. But there wouldn't be any television at all until she got this place cleaned up and decorated.

She set about wiping down the walls, doorframes, and windowsills with a damp cloth. She could only imagine when the last time this place was cleaned. When she came to one of the living room windows, she realized she could see right into Grumpy's house.

He was lying on a couch, his head back and eyes closed. He looked peaceful. Cori found herself staring. He had a chiseled face with a strong jawline. A thick neck led down to broad, tattooed shoulders, and the intricate ink patterns continued down his chest and arms. They weren't in color like a lot of the tattoos she'd seen—instead, they were jet black and dipped and swirled like a never-ending stream. She wasn't sure where one piece ended and the next began. What's more, she had never seen a man with abs like his. They were the well-defined abs of a professional athlete. She wanted—desperately—to touch them.

She was rooted in place watching him…until his eyes opened. They instantly roved her way. Without thinking, she dropped down to her hands and knees. *Oh god.* Did he see her watching him? Her heart was racing. After a moment on the floor, she felt absolutely ridiculous. What kind of grown woman does that? That thought didn't, however, stop her from crawling away from the window before she stood up again. Entering her kitchen, she casually looked toward the window she had cowardly abandoned.

Grumpy stood in his window, his hands braced above his head. He stood there as if he was on display. If someone asked her to describe the word "sex," she would give every tantalizing detail about the man currently gazing her way.

Determined not to let him get to her, Cori continued with her cleaning. By the time she had finished the first floor, she was exhausted. The upstairs could wait until tomorrow.

She placed an order for a pizza at a local mom-and-pop shop. Figuring she had a good thirty minutes, she ran upstairs to shower before it arrived.

Cori felt refreshed by the time the young woman arrived with her dinner. The smell of pizza sauce and melted cheese made her mouth water and her stomach growl. She sat at the kitchen table as she ate the gooey yumminess, looking out at her backyard. She could already picture the garden she was anxious to plant. Gardening always gave her a sense of peace. It was a relaxing hobby in her hectic world.

Now that she had something in her stomach, she needed to take a ride to the mall and the grocery store. She couldn't live on takeout alone, and she needed curtains for her bedroom. The ones she had packed from her previous apartment wouldn't fit here. Cori quickly cleaned up her mess and stored the leftovers in the refrigerator.

She locked the door before closing it behind her. Cori stole a glance over at her neighbor's house. A single light illuminated the living room. She got into her car and backed out of her driveway. She had other things to do beside think of a certain man.

———

When Cori pulled into her driveway, she was exhausted. A long day of cleaning followed by an evening of shopping was enough to wear any woman out. After gathering her packages, she carried everything into the house and straight up the stairs to her bedroom, since almost everything she'd bought was for her master suite, anyway.

As she began to put things away, she noticed her bathroom door was slightly ajar and the light was on. She stood there staring as she mentally retraced her steps before she'd left the house. She didn't remember turning the light on at all.

She slowly inched her way to the door and hesitantly pushed it open all the way. Inside, the vanity mirror had been shattered; shards of reflective glass littered the floor. The toilet paper was shredded like confetti all over the room. Above the sink, scrawled on the wall, was a message. Or perhaps a warning?

You can't hide

She backed out of the room, dazed and confused at the destruction. Cori tripped over the bedroom rug and screamed as she fell hard on her ass. Who would do this to her? She didn't know anyone in town. In fact, the only person she had met lived next door.

A loud bang shook the entire house, like a bomb had been detonated nearby. The sound scared the hell out of her. Were they under attack? Cori still hadn't regained her train of thought, so there she sat on her bedroom floor as Grumpy barged into her room. He'd traded his basketball shorts for jeans and tan work boots, but his chest was still distractingly naked. A baseball cap adorned his head, obscuring his eyes in shadows.

She looked up at him. "Excuse me?" she squeaked. "What are you doing in my house?"

"I heard you scream." His eyes searched the room suspiciously before landing back on her. "Are you all right?'

He stretched his hand out to her. She accepted the offer, and his hand completely dwarfed hers. Then again, everything about him dwarfed her. He pulled her up to her feet. She brushed her behind off, more out of habit than necessity. She found herself eye level with his sculpted chest. A naked, yummy chest. Would he flinch if she traced one of his tats with her tongue?

He snapped his fingers an inch from her face. "Hey… Are you all right?" he repeated.

"Yeah, sorry. I think…well, I think someone broke in while I was out today."

He raised an eyebrow. "You *think* or they *did*?"

She scrubbed her hands over her face. "They did." She pointed to her bathroom. "In there."

He charged into the adjoining room. Cori waited for him to emerge. It didn't take long.

He exited the bathroom, glaring at her. "Are you in some kind of trouble?"

She glared back. "No." This was the last thing she needed. All she wanted was a shower—obviously not in *that* bathroom tonight—and some sleep.

"Be honest with me, Cori."

She put her hands on her hips. "I said no, and I don't like the tone you're using." It was nearly impossible to be intimidating toward a man who looked as if he could break her in half.

"Look, I know you're new around here. I don't know how things were wherever you came from, but around here we look out for our neighbors. We also look out for ourselves. I need to know if a shit storm is brewing next to me."

Cori scowled at him. "You're a dick."

His smile stretched from ear to ear. "That's one of the nicer names I've been called, sweetheart."

"Don't 'sweetheart' me." He was incredibly aggravating. "I'm as clueless as you are, as to who did this." She waved her hand wildly in the direction of the bathroom. Okay, so maybe that was a *little* white lie…it could be a certain grieving widower. But she couldn't blame someone for a crime with no proof. No one knew where she had moved to except her previous landlord and her sister, Brianna.

Maybe the vandal mistook her for someone else? Maybe they didn't realize someone new had moved into the place? Yeah, that also seemed unlikely. She really didn't know the man currently scowling at her, so she wasn't going to divulge that information just yet. Who was she to dismiss him as the culprit? A new neighbor prank of sorts. Even as the thought formed, though, she mentally rolled her eyes. There was no way it was him. Not with the way he'd stormed her house with concern etched on his face. Now, however, the concern had been replaced by distrust.

"You're lying," he said. "To both me and yourself. I don't know why or what you're hiding, but I can see each thought flit across your pretty little face." He shrugged and turned on his heel toward the door. "Whatever—I'll quick fix your front door for tonight. Tomorrow I'll replace it."

Her mouth hung slightly agape. "You broke my front door? What the hell were you thinking?" Her voice rose with every word.

"You were screaming. I reacted. It's what I do. Like I said, I'll fix it."

"Neanderthal," she whispered.

He grinned at her before slipping out of her room. She could feel her cheeks flush from nothing more than a smile from him. She was frozen there, staring at the place where he'd stood a moment ago. The sound of his boots on her hardwood steps jolted her. Stomping her foot like a toddler, she followed him downstairs.

The front door still stood open. Splinters of wood littered the floor. The door frame had been completely busted. *What the hell?* She looked around the room. He was nowhere in sight. She stomped outside, putting so much force in her steps that the bottoms of her feet actually stung. Her arms swinging with purpose, she came to a halt. Cori scanned the area. She spotted him halfway across the yard. Crossing her arms over her chest, she marched after him.

"What the hell did you do to my door?"

"Really? The door again? I told you, I broke it," he called over his shoulder.

"With what? A battering ram?"

"My foot."

"Same difference," she scoffed. "Care to tell me how you plan on fixing it?"

He stopped walking and turned around to face her. "Well, you have a usable back door. Therefore, I'm going to nail the front door closed until the stores open tomorrow." He spoke to her like she was a crazy person—slowly and clearly. "Then I'll go get what I need to repair it properly. Meanwhile, you may want to contact the BCPD. If this turns out to be something, you want everything documented." He continued to his backyard.

She knew he was right; she wished he wasn't. If anyone knew the importance of reporting things of this nature, it would be her. How many patients had she counseled to do the same thing and they'd refused? It only made matters worse when things escalated beyond their control. On rare occasions, silence had deadly consequences.

"Thank you," she choked out when he returned.

"Don't mention it." He tipped his baseball cap as he carried a large board in the direction of her house.

Her arms dropped to her sides. Feeling defeated, she entered the living room behind him. Paxton closed the door, holding the board in place with his forearm. He held the nail in place, then used his other hand to hammer it home. He added two more nails before moving to the other end of the board. He repeated his actions there.

She liked watching him. The way his muscles moved, almost gracefully, was a sight to behold. She always did like a man who could work with his hands.

With the board secured in place for the evening, he turned to face her. She felt her stomach quiver, and her pulse sped up. She hated that he affected her this way.

He stalked over to her and stopped just inches away from touching her. She *wanted* him to touch her. Cori's fingers itched to touch him too. She wondered what his muscles would feel like under her palms. She wanted to trace one of his tattoos with her fingertips. Hell, she wanted to trace them all. Her pulse continued to speed up at an alarming rate as she gazed up at him.

"Lock the back door behind me. I'll be back in the morning."

Without waiting for her to reply, he walked away. She stood there trying to catch her breath and regain her composure. Remembering the lock, she ran toward the kitchen and the back door. She screamed again. Outside, Grumpy's frame filled the window in the door. He shook his head while laughing at her. Pointing to the lock she hadn't yet engaged, he watched her approach the door. Her eyes never left his as she slowly reached out toward the door. The metal from the deadbolt chilled her fingertips. She knew once she flipped the lock, he would be gone.

Just like that, she was alone. The house felt eerie with him gone, which was insane—she'd just met the man. Sighing, she checked each room again. She double checked all the windows and inspected the front door. She had a mess to clean upstairs.

She took pictures with her phone first to document the destruction, but she didn't want to involve the police unless it was absolutely necessary. Hopefully this was an isolated event. She was exhausted and just wanted to go to sleep…at least she hoped she could after all of this.

THREE
TANK

PAXTON FLOPPED ONTO HIS COUCH, pulling his laptop to him. Cori was lying to him about something, he just knew it, and he was determined to find out more about her. When it came to technology, he was perfectly capable of simple background checks. This time, however, he wanted everything he could get on this woman. That meant calling in the big guns. Retrieving his phone from the coffee table, he dialed the one guy who could find out anything he wanted about someone.

"Tank, what's up?" Mother answered cheerfully.

"Hey, man. I need you to look into someone for me. Her name is Cori Transue. See what you can find on her."

"A woman? I don't recall any of our cases involving a woman with that name. Is she involved with Petrov?"

Crime boss Lupis Petrov was currently on his deathbed. Paxton and the rest of the guys were still looking for his coward of a son, Ivan, who had gone underground after trying to kill Max's girlfriend, Sloane. She had worked for a very powerful man, Detlef Marek. Unfortunately, he owed that power to the Petrov family.

When Ivan came to collect, Detlef had since grown a conscience. Obviously that didn't end well, and he was murdered right before Sloane's eyes, putting her in the Petrov family's crosshairs.

"Not Petrov. She's my new neighbor. Something is going on with her."

"You becoming a little old lady now? Sittin' at home, spyin' on the neighbors?" Mother laughed. "Sounds like you've got too much time on your hands, big man."

"Kiss my big hairy ass, Mother. Someone broke into her place tonight. There was a small amount of vandalism. She claims she doesn't know anyone who would do it, but my gut tells me she's lying."

"We all know you always listen to your gut. How deep do you want me to go?"

"Find out where she's from. Whatever skeletons are in her closet that could come back and haunt her."

Paxton could hear Mother's fingers flying over his keyboard. It only took him a few minutes to do what would have taken Paxton hours.

"She's twenty-nine years old. Parents, deceased. One younger sister, Brianna. Never been married and no kids. Damn, this chick is a doctor too."

"What kind of doctor?" Paxton asked.

"Shrink. Hold up." Mother paused for a moment. Paxton could hear the tapping of the keys again. "Looks like there's a lawsuit filed against her. Just a few weeks ago too."

"She's being sued? For what? By who?" Paxton barked impatiently into the phone.

"Chill the fuck out, bro. I'm reading. Okay, looks like a patient committed suicide. Our girl is being sued for wrongful death by the grieving husband."

Paxton could feel his blood boiling. "Any truth?" Even though he had just met her, he couldn't imagine her being responsible for someone's death. Knowing someone out there was blaming her pissed him off.

"According to these documents, no. He's just looking to cash in."

"Great."

"So who's this woman to you?" Mother asked again.

Even though Mother couldn't see him, Paxton rolled his eyes. "I told you, she's my neighbor."

His friend chuckled. "Uh huh."

"If you come up with anything else, let me know."

Paxton ended the call. There was nothing going on with Cori, and there wasn't going to be. That didn't mean he couldn't look out for her, though. He may not be a cop anymore, but the instinct to protect was still there in full force. He paced over to the same window he'd caught her watching him through earlier.

He scanned the yard. No one lurked in the shadows, and all her lights were out. It seemed as though she was settled for the night. Paxton decided he should probably turn in himself. He had to go to the hardware store in the morning. After turning off his laptop and television, he dragged himself upstairs.

———

The sun was barely kissing the horizon as Paxton swung his legs over the side of the bed. His knee ached like a bitch today. Scrubbing his hands over his scruffy face, he tried to wake up. When he felt his motor skills were awake enough to keep him from walking into any walls, he strolled naked into the bathroom. After he relieved himself, he brushed his teeth and entered the shower. The hot water sluiced off the rest of his sleepiness.

With nothing more than a towel wrapped around his waist, he went down to the kitchen to make coffee. He pulled a single-serving pod from the cabinet, put it into the machine, and waited. A few moments later, he had a steaming mug full of black coffee. He lifted the cup to his face, breathing in the aroma before taking a sip. The hot liquid instantly rejuvenated him. As he padded through the house to go get dressed, he stopped in the living room to check his phone. Out of the corner of his eye, he noticed movement.

He opened the camera on his phone. Flipping it to video, he held it up in front of himself. With the phone in a selfie position, he used it to look over his shoulder. Once again, he found Cori in her window watching him. He felt the smile spread across his face. She liked to watch him. *Hmm.* Maybe he should give her something to look at? Paxton reached down with his other hand and dropped his towel. His eyes never left the screen that was now recording Cori's reaction.

Her hand covered her mouth in surprise. He couldn't stop himself from cracking up. It was the first time a woman had made him laugh so candidly, other than Max's daughter, in a long time. Since Mia was only a few months old, he didn't think she counted as a woman, though.

He could see the red blossom across her cheeks as she stood there staring. Her eyes locked onto his ass. Suddenly, she snapped out of her stupor. She looked around suspiciously before scurrying away from the window. Stopping the recording, he continued—naked— up to his room. He laughed the entire way.

Dressed in a pair of blue jeans and a gray t-shirt,

Paxton left his house, locking the front door behind him. He glanced over at Cori's window as he climbed into his truck. It was vacant.

The trip to the store was a quick one. He bought a new door, locks, and molding to fix the mess he'd made. In his defense, she'd been screaming like a damn banshee. He loaded everything into the bed of his truck. The whole excursion only took him a little over an hour. Hopefully she was awake so he could get started. Since the front door to Cori's place was still boarded up, he traipsed around to the back door.

She was in the kitchen emptying boxes that littered the table. She looked cute as hell with her hair pulled back as she worked on the mess covering the countertops.

He rapped on the door, smiling as she jumped. Her hand covered her heart, while a cute scowl formed on her face. Smiling, he held up his drill. This time she didn't meet his gaze when she turned the lock. He was slightly disappointed, which surprised him. She opened the door and moved aside for him to enter.

"Good morning, sweetheart. What, no breakfast?"

She rolled her eyes at him. "It's too early for your shit, Paxton." She shut the door and went back to the box she had been going through. "I hope you're here to fix my busted door."

"Well, I'm certainly not here for your sparkling conversational skills this morning." He continued to smile at her. "It's gonna be a little noisy. I have to fix the frame and re-drill. I bought you a new lock too. That other one was a piece of shit."

Paxton tried not to notice how great her ass looked in the blue yoga pants she was wearing. He did not succeed. He just knew she'd look amazing bent over the kitchen island, with his fresh handprint pink on her ass cheek. Shaking his head clear of the image, he left the kitchen to fix the door.

He put all his supplies down except his hammer. It was time to get started. Pulling the nails out of his barricade, he tried to keep his mind on the task at hand.

He had the old door removed and the new one in place when his cell phone began ringing in his back pocket. He pulled it free and pressed the green answer button on the screen. He put it on speaker so he could keep working on the new lock. He could hear a lot of commotion in the background.

Gutter Mouth's voice boomed through the speaker. "Whatcha up to, motherfucker?"

He chuckled in response. "You kiss your mother with that mouth, asshole?"

Kasper, aka Gutter Mouth, had the most vulgar vocabulary of anyone Paxton had ever met. That included cracked-out junkies and his many military buddies. Paxton loved the guy. He had ever since they were know-it-all teenagers causing trouble every chance they got. Gutter Mouth never failed to make him laugh.

"Only yours, bitch." Kiss noises came through the line loud and clear. "Seriously, Tank. What the fuck are you doing? I thought you were coming in today."

Paxton continued to put in the new lock as he talked. "Fixing my neighbor's door. Are you at the office?"

"Yeah, but that's no longer important. What neighbor and why are you fixing their door?"

"Because Grumpy kicked it in last night." Cori startled him from the doorway. Her shoulder rested casually against the door jam, and one foot was crossed over the other. She was exquisite. He had an unusual urge to go to her. He needed to get his head back in the game.

"Well," Gutter Mouth drawled. "Hello there, darlin'. Who do I have the pleasure of speaking to?"

Cori laughed. "Cori, the new neighbor. And you are?" she asked playfully. Was she enjoying Gutter Mouth's banter? She never sounded so flirty with him. *What the fuck?*

"Kasper. Hasn't my buddy Tank told you about me yet? Tank, you holding out on me, man?"

"Shut the fuck up, Gutter Mouth."

Her eyebrow arched in question. "Tank? Gutter Mouth?"

Gutter Mouth kept talking. "As you can see, my friend there is built like a fucking tank. And well...I'm sure you've guessed where my nickname came from." Gutter Mouth's laughter echoed through the speaker.

Paxton spoke through a clenched jaw. "Hanging up now, asshole. I'll be in later." He hung up and his gaze landed on Cori yet again. "Sorry about him."

She looked at him as if deep in thought. "Tank...It's fitting."

"Yeah, well. It could be worse," he grumbled.

She smiled sweetly. "I'm sure it could."

"I'm almost done here, then I'll be out of your hair." He sat on his haunches after putting the second-to-last screw into place. He had to get away from her before he did something stupid.

"Thank you." Her eyes dropped to her feet. "I should have said that last night."

He stopped what he was doing and stood up. "Don't do that," he ordered firmly.

Her gaze darted up to his. "Do what?"

"Lose all that sass you've been throwing at me. The pensive look doesn't suit you."

Her body language changed instantly. Her back straightened and she glared at him. "And it's good to see *you* again, Mr. Dick Weasel."

Cori stomped out of the room as he roared with laughter. She was sexy as fuck when she was rattled. Paxton wanted to rattle her more. As he finished up the door, a wave of disappointment washed over him. He was done and therefore had no excuse to be around her. He wanted an excuse, damn it.

"Shake it off," he mumbled.

She peeked her head around the corner. "You call me?"

"Better than new." He pointed to the door and its shiny new lock.

She smirked. "It's about time."

"That's my girl." He threw her a wink as he gathered his tools. Her face flushed at his slip of tongue. He liked that. He liked that a lot.

———

"About time you showed up." Gutter Mouth spun in his office chair like a five-year-old.

He flipped his best friend the bird. "Yeah, you look swamped."

"Suck me."

Sloane hustled over to him, throwing her arms around his neck. She was a little thing. Then again, Paxton could say that about most women. She had long, honey blonde hair and a smile that was contagious. She squeezed him tighter before stepping back to look up at him. She pushed her bangs out of her face, smiling up at him.

"Tank, how you doing, hon?"

He grinned. "Better since I saw your beautiful smile."

"I wish you assholes would all stop flirting with my wife," Max bellowed as he entered the room.

Gutter Mouth ejected himself from his chair like a rocket taking flight. He grabbed up Sloane in his arms, turning their bodies so he blocked her from view. He looked like one of those cheesy villains in the old movies that kidnaps the hero's girl and ties her to the railroad tracks.

Gutter Mouth grinned at Max. "She's not the little woman yet, Maxie Pad. There's still time for her to change her mind." He turned his head toward her. "Whatcha say, darlin'? Ready to run away with me yet?"

Max fixed Gutter Mouth with a death stare. "Get your hands off my woman," he ordered through clenched teeth.

Sloane laughed. "Kasper, don't get him riled up." She slapped his arm playfully.

He winked. "You'll thank me later."

Paxton chuckled again. Max had been overprotective of Sloane from day one. They all had an immense amount of fun teasing him about it, but Paxton was happy his friend had found love. Real love. You could see it in the way they looked at each other. He thought he'd had that once, with Gillian. He'd been happy. He'd thought she'd been happy too, but it was all a lie. She'd been carrying on with other men for longer than he'd imagined. He'd been a cop and still hadn't seen the evidence until the relationship was already over.

He wasn't going to go through that again. No way. No woman was worth that amount of pain. One night—that's all he was willing to offer anyone. He thought of Cori, but dismissed it just as quickly. That wasn't going to happen.

She wasn't that type of woman. She was the type of woman who wanted it all, he could tell. A cry from the back room momentarily silenced everyone.

"Sounds like Mia is awake from her nap. Excuse me, boys." Sloane left the room, heading to the back room toward the soft cries.

All the guys at Fear Incorporated thought of Sloane and Mia as theirs too. Sloane cooked for them more often than she should've, and Max always told them to get their own women. Paxton always laughed at that. They were all playboys—that wouldn't happen anytime soon. Instead, Mia had five incredibly large "uncles" that would make the perfect repellant for any future teenage boys who thought they could take advantage of her.

Paxton took a seat at his desk. The new office still smelled faintly of paint. There were six desks set up around the room—his was in the back next to Gutter Mouth's, while the other desks were occupied by Mother, Benji, Max, and Sloane. Max was talking to Mother at his desk, Gutter Mouth had disappeared, and it had been almost a year since they'd last seen Benji.

He pulled up his inbox, not expecting to find much, if anything. The office had only been open a few weeks. Today was his first day. Anything important and any new jobs would go to Max and Sloane to divvy out.

With no case of his own yet, he made a list of all the things he needed to pick up later. Max would order any office supplies he needed, but Paxton wanted little things to make his space his. Those things he would pick up this weekend for himself. Mother walked over to his desk.

"Tank, I ran the widower's credit cards and bank account. There's no record of him being in Bush Castle. Although…he used his credit card about twenty miles out of town a few days ago. Either he went back home or he just hasn't had the need to use his cards, and I'm not ruling out him using cash yet."

"Thanks, Mother."

"I'll check traffic cameras in the area around the time of the incident. Maybe we'll get lucky."

"I owe ya one. Hey, anything new on Petrov?"

"The father is on his deathbed. Baby boy, Ivan, still hasn't emerged from hiding yet. I've been keeping a watch on his electronic trail. Benji is still beating the pavement. He sends encrypted emails whenever he can to keep us updated."

Benjamin Agani spent most of his time out of the office; he'd been an undercover officer while with the police force. When shit went down with Sloane, he took up his undercover persona once again to gather as much information as he could to help them, this time for Fear Incorporated. He was a master at blending in and had eyes and ears all over. That he couldn't find Ivan, the next heir of the Petrov crime family, had pissed him off. He'd been looking nonstop for eighteen months—he even missed Mia's birth because he'd had a lead that turned into nothing but a dead end.

Paxton groaned. "Fuck."

"We'll find him. Once we do and the father bites it, our girls will be safe."

"The sooner the better. I'm surprised he's been able to fly under the radar for this long."

Paxton glanced toward movement coming from the back. He scurried over to a baby-toting Sloane. Snatching the little girl from her mother, he tossed her up in the air. His heart melted from her delightful squeals. "How's my best girl today?"

She giggled, drooling slightly. He didn't care. He'd do anything just to hear her laugh. She sounded like an angel.

"You guys are gonna spoil her rotten."

Paxton kissed Mia's little hand that was wrapped around his finger. She babbled away about something. "That's what uncles are for, to spoil their beautiful nieces."

"Hand her over." Gutter Mouth reached out for the squirmy little girl.

Kissing Mia's forehead, he relinquished her to his best friend. He made it all the way back to his desk before Sloane started the inquisition. Frankly, he was surprised it had taken her this long.

"So, Tank." She moseyed over to him. A sly little smile tugged at her lips. "Who's the new neighbor?"

He feigned innocence. "A woman who recently moved in next door."

She frowned at him, her hands resting on her hips. "Don't be a smartass. What's her name? What's she like? Is she married? Single? Boyfriend?" Sloane's excitement reminded him of a little kid trying to guess at their birthday present.

"Cori. Her name is Cori. She's not married. She's a voyeuristic, stubborn, pain in the ass," he grumbled under his breath.

Sloane gasped. She did nothing to hide the surprised look on her face. "You like her." She wasn't asking. She was telling him.

He waved her off. "Don't be silly. I barely know the woman."

"According to Mother, you know a lot about her now. And did I catch a voyeur comment in there?" She giggled. "What was she watching?"

Paxton smiled up at her from his seat. "I'd show you, but Max would lose his shit."

"Oh my god, Tank." Sloane covered her mouth to staunch her laughter. She stopped laughing and her face became worried. "Seriously, what's going on? Is she in trouble?"

He narrowed his eyes. "Honestly, I'm not sure yet. My gut says something's up. So I'm trying to find out."

"Oh, boy. Anything I can do to help?"

Sloane was as sweet as they came. She was always looking out for them or trying to make things easier on them. He guessed it was her way of paying them back for watching out for her and now Mia. It was completely unnecessary, but that's just who she was. "Nah, but I'll let you know if that changes."

"Fair enough." She kissed the top of his head and walked away.

Max was certainly a lucky man. He watched Sloane pluck her daughter from Gutter Mouth's grasp, much to his chagrin. Max crossed the room, taking both of them into his arms. He beamed down at them, his expression no less than extreme joy. Paxton felt that familiar pang of jealousy.

Not that he wanted Sloane. She was amazing, but not for him. He pictured himself with a giggling, raven-haired baby girl...

Whoa. That was enough of that nonsense.

He swiveled his chair back to face his computer. There had to be something to keep his mind off a certain pain-in-the-ass woman. These thoughts were complete bullshit.

FOUR
LUKE

ANGER FESTERED as he watched the man from next door fix Cori's front door. He didn't like that her neighbor was inserting himself into Cori's life. Luke already had plans for her—she was going to belong with *him*. He deserved it, and she owed it to him. For the past two days, he'd been watching her, waiting for the moment when he could make his move.

She was more beautiful than he'd remembered. Luke rubbed his hands together in anticipation. He couldn't wait to have her.

But first, she had to suffer. He had it all arranged. Once she paid for taking his sweet Becky, she would take her place. He wondered if she'd fight when he made her wear the collar; Becky did the first few times. But by the fourth, she'd learned her place.

Cori was probably a fighter. He would enjoy breaking her.

The neighbor finally went back to his own damn house, Cori watching from the window. He sneered. Every time

Luke thought he'd have the perfect moment, Bigfoot from next door would show up. He'd even noticed the man scanning the property at night. Talk about paranoid.

This wasn't going to be as easy as he'd originally thought. He was going to need some time to think.

FIVE
CORI

NOW THAT HER door was fixed, Cori gathered her things to head over to the home improvement store. She spent over an hour debating between two different sheds to replace the firewood that was there now. In the end, she went with a medium-size one that resembled a barn and had a window to allow for ventilation.

After setting up delivery for her new shed, she swiftly made her way over to the gardening section. She pored over the flowers, thinking of what would look best around the front porch.

She was in love with flowers of all kinds. She found some beautiful peonies, tulips, and daffodils. Once her cart was full of flowers, she put the necessary amount of soil and mulch in the bottom of the cart. Cori found an open register and paid for her purchases. She couldn't wait to get home and get started on transforming her yard.

It took almost a dozen trips from her car to the porch to unload her goodies. Then she bounded inside and changed her clothes. Pulling on a pair of cut-off denim shorts and a tank top, she grabbed her gardening tools and started in the front yard. It took her a couple of hours to get the front flower beds the way she had envisioned them. Once she was done, it was beautiful.

When she came around to the backyard, she didn't think anything of the long white box on the table until she realized it was a flower box. Excitement flooded her. Could they be from a certain grumpy neighbor? She berated herself—there was no reason he would leave her flowers. Absolutely none. She was being ridiculous. But as ridiculous as it was, she still hoped.

She recalled this morning, when she'd glanced out her window and noticed him standing there on his phone in nothing except a towel. She couldn't take her eyes from his sculpted back. Tattoos adorned his shoulder blades, but the rest of his back was bare. Then, Lord help her, the white fluffy-looking towel slipped from his hips. She'd covered her mouth to keep herself from squealing. The finest ass she'd ever laid eyes on was on display for her viewing pleasure.

He'd continued to play with his phone a few moments longer, the muscles twitching in his legs and butt as he moved his weight around. Cori tried not to drool on herself. She barely managed such a herculean feat, but then she'd realized someone could be watching her watch him. Mortified, she backed away from the window. From a safe distance, she watched him put his phone down and for one brief moment, she'd thought she could see the outline of his penis. *There's no way*, she had told herself. That would make it...*wow*. She hadn't been able to think straight again until after he'd disappeared.

Shit, if anything, she should send *him* flowers after that. Ones with large stems. She giggled to herself as she untied the red ribbon from the stark white box. Inside, black roses mocked her, the petals plucked from their stems and lining the bottom of the box. A picture of her accompanied the disassembled flowers. With trembling fingers, she picked it up. It was taken outside of her house. In the photograph, she was wearing the same cut-offs and tank top she had on right now.

There was a poorly drawn red heart framing her image. He had been here today. She dropped the photo back into the box and scanned her surroundings.

She felt like she couldn't breathe. Her heart pounded in her chest, and her throat tightened up. Every sound commanded her attention. Her eyes searched the yard she'd felt so safe in just moments ago—moments before she knew for a fact that someone had been watching her. Maybe they still were.

Panicked, she ran into the house. She checked to make sure all the doors and windows were locked before she phoned the authorities. She curled herself into a ball in the corner of her couch, her cell phone clutched in her hand in case she needed it. A half hour went by and still no red and blue lights in her driveway. What she did see, however, was Paxton marching quickly up her front porch steps, his hands fisted tightly at his sides. She swallowed hard. It looked like he was back to being Grumpy. She jumped up from the couch and ran to the door, which she opened before he could knock. She stood with one hand on the door, the other on her hip.

"To what do I owe the honor?" she asked calmly, hoping he didn't notice how shaken up she was.

His arm shot out and snaked around her waist as he whisked her inside, kicking the door closed behind him. She wasn't sure what startled her more—the thud of the door or his arm wrapped tightly around her. Her breath hitched as his muscled chest pressed deliciously against hers. She had to remember how to speak with him touching her that way.

"What the hell, Tank?" she asked breathlessly.

He stopped with his mouth slightly agape. She realized she had used the nickname his friends used. Was he upset? She really hadn't meant to; it just sorta slipped out. He twisted her up inside. She didn't like it. Not one bit.

She wrenched herself from his embrace, snatched a laundry basket full of clean clothes from next to the coffee table, and stomped upstairs with them. She needed to be doing something with her hands before she made an ass out of herself by attacking him. She could feel him following closely behind her.

"Where's the box?"

She sighed. "I left it where I found it—outside."

"Good."

She stopped in the landing. Spinning around, she glared at him. "I'm not stupid, ya know."

"I wasn't insinuating you were."

"Could've fooled me."

She twirled on her heel, carrying the basket into her room. The basket dropped to the floor with a thud, and a scream tore from her lips. Turning to run out of the room, she slammed into the hard chest behind her. She buried her face into his soft cotton shirt and inhaled the scent of him, musky and mouthwatering. It was intoxicating even as she held onto him and cried.

"Fucking hell," he whispered.

His arms enveloped her. Like a cage, she was trapped. It was an amazing feeling to be engulfed in his arms, his scent teasing her nostrils. She felt her core tighten. Paxton picked her up and propelled them into the hallway. Setting her down at arm's length, he frowned at her.

"No more fucking games, Cori. This shit is serious now."

Cori knew it was serious. She was the one with a dead animal in her bed. The poor thing had been so thoroughly mangled, she couldn't even tell what it once was. Blood and tufts of fur covered the sheets. There was no way she was sleeping on that mattress ever again. Her room felt tainted—she had to get out of there.

She pressed her hands to her stomach, hoping it would staunch the nauseous feeling swirling inside of her. "Can we please have this discussion downstairs or even better, outside?"

Paxton shook his head. "I don't think it's smart to stand outside for this discussion. Let's go over to my place."

"Okay." She would have agreed to anything to get out of there. He followed her back down the steps and out the front door. She turned back to grab her house keys.

Like he had read her mind, he jingled her keys between his fingers. "I've got 'em." She was so out of it, she didn't even see him grab them.

She kept herself from running across their yards through sheer will and determination. She didn't want an outsider to think she'd been shaken. If her new friend was still watching her, she didn't want to give him the satisfaction of seeing her spooked. But who was she trying to kid? Spooked? She was *terrified*.

Paxton reached out, opening the screen door in front of her. She moved to the side so he could unlock the heavy wooden inside door. Cori inched her way inside. The walls of his living room were a creamy gray with white trim. She recognized the slate blue couch she had watched him sleep on just yesterday morning. He shut the door behind them and moved farther into the room.

He sat down on the couch, patting the space beside him. She was nervous to sit so close after the way his touch affected her earlier. She eyed the recliner before telling herself to just sit down. She was being ridiculous. Tentatively, she approached him. She lowered herself onto the soft, worn fabric. Her pulse raced. She wasn't sure if it was from the fear of someone stalking her or from the memory of being in his embrace minutes ago. She was betting on both.

"How did you know? About the flowers?" She rubbed her hands across the denim of her pants absentmindedly.

"I have friends in the Sherriff's office."

Caught off guard by his response, she lifted her gaze to meet his. "Are you a cop?"

"Not anymore."

Intrigued, she focused on his face. "What happened?"

"Injury. It was a few years ago." His tone dismissed that particular line of questioning. It only made her more curious. Something she would have to revisit later. Without thinking, Cori reached out, laying a comforting hand on his knee.

"I'm sorry," she whispered.

Their eyes locked. Her breath hitched. His massive hand covered hers. She felt small and fragile next to him, and she liked feeling that way. Like a cobra, his other hand snaked around the back of her head. He pulled her to him, their lips a breath apart. Butterflies attacked her stomach in droves. A sly, mischievous grin spread across his lips a second before they crashed down onto hers.

Cori's body came aflame. His tongue pushed past her lips, and spearmint exploded in her mouth as his talented tongue caressed hers. He sucked her bottom lip in between plunges, and she felt that suction all the way down to her core. She instantly wondered if he would devour the rest of her with such enthusiasm. Her panties were completely drenched from nothing more than a kiss—a kiss she feared she would use as a comparison for all future kisses. She couldn't imagine one better.

She was ready. This man could take her right here, right now, and damn the consequences. Damn what tomorrow would bring. Nothing mattered except this blissfully perfect moment. The anticipation for him to touch her was bound to kill her if he waited much longer…and then there it was. His hand left hers, landing on her hip. She was so consumed her ears began to buzz.

Abruptly, he pulled away. Confused, she watched him pull his cell from his pocket. *Oh.* So it wasn't her ears buzzing, but his cell phone. He'd stopped to answer his *phone*?

He looked as if nothing had happened. What the hell *had* just happened?

"Yeah?" he spoke into the phone, his gaze fixed on her with an impassive expression.

She needed to put some space between them. "Restroom?" she mouthed.

He pointed down the hallway off the living room. She strayed down the dark corridor until she found the bathroom. Closing the door drowned out Tank's voice. Leaning back against the door, she touched her fingers to her lips. They felt tender to the touch, like she'd been branded by him. She pushed away from the door and looked at herself in the mirror. Her eyes were slightly glazed and her lips looked red and swollen. She had never been kissed that way before.

She touched her lips again. She was in major trouble. How was she going to get through the rest of the night?

SIX
TANK

WHAT THE FUCK had he been thinking? Did he or did he not decide just *yesterday* that Cori was a no-go? She was off limits. If Foster hadn't called him to let him know he was outside of her house with a few guys, there's no doubt he would've fucked her just now.

Damn, the way that woman responded to his touch was magical. Like a livewire. He still couldn't get his cock to calm down. He couldn't help but wonder how long it had been since a man had touched her.

He stood from the couch, walking off the excess energy he could feel crackling under his skin. Was she getting to him? Impossible—he didn't let women get to him. He plucked a bottle of water from the fridge. He stood with the door open, hoping the cool air would chill his dick the fuck out. He chugged the bottle down.

Cori emerged from the bathroom a few minutes later, her lips swollen and red. Paxton felt like strutting around the living room like a peacock, knowing *he'd* put that glow on her face.

It was absurd. He'd never once felt a sense of pride after fucking a girl. Just the opposite, in fact. Why the hell would he, after a kiss? An amazing kiss, but still just a kiss. He needed to nip this in the bud and fast. He was nothing if not honest with the women he brought home. They knew where they stood and they were okay with it. He needed to set things straight with Cori before he hurt her. He didn't want her to think this was the beginning of something. It wasn't.

Cori wasn't anything like those women, because she didn't know how impossible it was for him to let himself get close to anyone again. The women he spent time with were just as damaged and guarded as he was. They wanted the same thing he did—a little comfort for a few hours. Nothing more. She was better than what he had to offer.

She flashed him a smile bright enough to light up the darkest day. It was stunning. It only made him feel like more of an ass.

"I need to apologize."

She raised an eyebrow. "Apologize?" Confusion was evident in her voice.

"I shouldn't have kissed you. I'm sorry. I don't know what I was thinking."

The smile slipped slowly from her lips. She wrapped her arms around herself. He shouldn't have said anything. He should've just pretended like it hadn't happened at all. She turned her back to him.

He wanted to go to her. He wanted to wrap his arms around her, but he knew that was the opposite of what he should do. He could tell by her body language that she was hurt and embarrassed. He didn't want to make things worse. So he stood there.

"So…police are over at your place now," he muttered. "We, uh, should go talk to them."

"Okay," she whispered without turning around. Her steps were slow as she left his house.

The air outside was crisp and cool. He inhaled deeply, taking in the night air. He had to get her sweet scent out of his head. It reminded him of vanilla and lavender.

Officers traipsed in and out of the house next door, and he could hear others in the backyard, no doubt documenting the box of flowers. He scanned the street. Neighbors watched from their windows and front porches—the downside of small-town living. This would be top gossip for weeks to come.

He approached his friend. "Hey, man," he called. Foster gave him a shoulder hug. Paxton jerked his head toward the woman. "This is Cori."

Foster smiled and extended his hand. "Detective Foster Hyland, ma'am."

Cori accepted his handshake. "Dr. Cori Transue."

Foster pulled out a notebook, readying himself. "Can you recall the events of today, Doctor? Don't leave out any detail. The smallest thing could be helpful."

She shoved her hands in the front pockets of her shorts as she began the story of her day. She did however, leave out one detail: She didn't tell Foster she'd been watching Paxton stand in his living room in nothing more than his birthday suit. While she recounted her story, Foster jotted down notes on his pad.

"Once I found the flowers, I called the department. It wasn't until Paxton showed up that we found the… mess…upstairs."

"Tank mentioned that this wasn't the first incident?"

She sighed. "No, officer. I had another break-in. Just damage to the master bathroom."

Foster looked up at her. "You never reported it to law officials?"

"No. I had hoped it would be a one-time thing. I did take photos. Just in case."

"I'll need a copy of those."

"Sure thing." She handed over her cell phone to Foster.

Foster put the small notebook into his back pocket and accepted the phone. "We have a team dusting for prints and looking for other evidence. It may be a while before the house is clear for you to enter." His tone was apologetic.

"She'll be over at my place until you're done," Paxton announced.

Cori looked at him like he'd grown a second head. "No. That's okay, Paxton. I can go somewhere else until they're finished up. I don't want to impose any more than I already have."

She was trying to blow him off. He didn't miss the fact that she had called him "Paxton" this time instead of Tank. After the way he'd gone from hot to cold earlier, he couldn't blame her. He also knew she had nowhere else to go in this town and her sister lived over an hour away.

Foster watched their interaction with interest, evident by the slight smirk on his face. Tank would hear about this later for sure.

"You don't know anyone else in town, it's getting late, and you and I both know you won't be able to sleep in that house, much less that room, until the mattress is replaced," Paxton continued.

Her eyes widened. "I am not sleeping with you," she huffed with vehemence.

He laughed loudly. "Relax, sweetheart. I wasn't suggesting that. I have a spare room. I also have a truck to haul your mattress in. I'm trying to help. Nothing more, nothing less."

Her cheeks reddened. "Oh…"

Foster cleared his throat. "I'll give you a call when it's clear, Tank. Dr. Transue, if you think of anything else or you have questions, don't hesitate to call. If there are any other incidents, call immediately." He handed over his business card along with her cell phone.

Cori took the card and slipped it into her pocket. "Thank you, Detective."

Paxton thanked Foster before turning back toward his own home. He didn't say anything else to Cori. She'd come inside when she was ready. Besides, there were half a dozen cops to watch out for her.

Once inside, he took a seat on the couch and turned on his laptop. He'd replied to three emails by the time Cori joined him in the house. She looked lost. He wanted to kill the motherfucker responsible for putting that look on her face.

He watched her. "Are you okay?"

She nodded her head absentmindedly. "Fine, thanks."

He didn't believe that for a second, but he let it go. "I'll show you to your room."

Paxton rose from the couch, making sure not to touch her as he walked by. He didn't trust himself not to try to kiss her again. If he felt even a brush of her skin against his, he would lose the little bit of control he had left. He could hear her following behind him up to the top floor of the house. There were four bedrooms and a bathroom; he took her to the second master bedroom. It was slightly smaller than his, but it had its own bathroom and he figured that would make Cori feel a little more secure in his home.

"This is yours for the night. There's a bathroom with clean towels under the sink. It's only a stand-in shower, though. There's a full-size tub in the hall bathroom, if you prefer."

"Shower is fine." Her voice sounded hollow and sad.

"Okay, there are packaged soaps, toothbrushes, and plenty of shampoo in there. Also, there are some clothes in the drawer. Don't be shy about borrowing them. They should fit you, although the pants will probably be too long."

Her face lit up with the first spark of emotion he'd seen in hours, but it was quickly followed by a sneer. "Wow, you've thought of it all. I bet the women you bring home are grateful that you're *so* thoughtful afterwards," she spat.

He gritted his teeth. It pissed him off that she would make such an assumption without knowing anything about him. His baby sister came to stay with him for a few days on such a regular basis that he'd made this room permanently hers. Even though Krysta was five years younger than him, they were close. She was his best friend next to Gutter Mouth. She was like a livewire, whereas Paxton was more reserved.

Yet Cori had instantly thought he stocked supplies for the hordes of women he slept with. She didn't deserve an explanation. He pasted a wry smile on his face.

"The women who *come* here are extremely grateful, sweetheart."

Her mouth hung open slightly. She was cute. Not in a puppy dog way, but in a totally kissable kind of way. Paxton wanted to kiss her again. Common sense reminded him of what a shitty idea that was. Unfortunately, his libido overrode his common sense and he was once again consumed with the memory of their first kiss.

———

CORI

What an arrogant asshole. Cori couldn't believe her ears. She couldn't stand this man. No, that wasn't it. She couldn't stand the way he made her *feel*. He twisted her up inside just by looking at her. He stood there so smug, so sexy, she wanted to punch him. The suggestive way he'd said *come* had her mouth dropping open...both because she was floored he'd say such a thing to her and also because she could imagine him bringing her to the brink just before pushing her over.

His cocky smile begged for a response. Should she make a witty retort or insist he leave the room? Instead she grabbed a fist full of his shirt, pulling him down to her. She slid her lips over his, determined to counteract the effect of their earlier kiss. No one could make a person feel so much with one kiss, so it must've been a fluke.

Shit. She was wrong. So wrong. He pulled her closer, and she thought of the way he looked naked this morning. She wanted to taste every glorious inch of him.

Her arms locked around his neck as he lifted her ass in the air. Her body came crashing down onto the soft mattress, and Paxton pressed his hard body on top of her. He continued to kiss her. His hand cupped one of her breasts. It took her a moment to process the whimpering sound she kept hearing...then she realized she was making it. She hadn't been touched by a man in a long time. An *extremely* long time. The sensation was overpowering. She couldn't have stopped him even if she wanted to.

As much as she enjoyed kissing him, she wanted his mouth other places. There was a spot on her neck that would ruin her if he found it. She both feared and anticipated that moment.

His fingers traced down her body. A tug on her jeans pulled the button free. He didn't bother to unzip them. Again, he tugged—hard. Cori could hear the teeth of the zipper protest as it was wrenched open.

His palm was hot as it slid under the waistband of her shorts. Her body quivered from his touch. She was about to lose her mind. Then she felt him—a single finger traced over her wet lips. His mouth continued to caress, bite, and suck at her own. Paxton pushed inside of her. Her fingertips dug into his back.

He pulled back from their kiss and gazed down at her. She let her arms drop to the bed. His hand froze, the lone finger still inside her. Should she say something? Do something? She licked the taste of him off her swollen lips. He began moving his finger. She moaned, he moved faster. She gripped the sheets beneath her as the pleasure began to build.

Her breathing had become shallow. His thumb found her clit without missing a beat. He didn't continue kissing her. He watched as he brought her closer. Her moans turned into cries. Her body was alive in a way it hadn't ever been before. Not ever. It was only a finger. She felt herself stretch as he added a second finger. Cori cried out.

The orgasm hit her like a Mack truck. Starbursts exploded behind her closed eyes. She could feel him watching her, but she couldn't find the strength to care.

Wouldn't care, after he gave her this amazing gift. One she was eager to return as soon as she could feel her body again. He finally kissed her again. It was softer this time. Almost tender.

His face was seriously intense as he gazed down at her. "You're beautiful when you come."

Cori was too awestruck to answer him. He kissed her one last time before standing...she guessed to remove his clothes. Only he didn't remove anything—he walked to the bedroom door, then turned to face her. What looked like a pained expression quickly disappeared from his face. In its place was the cocky smile from earlier.

"You looked like you could use that. Try to get some sleep. I'll see you in the morning."

He pulled the door closed behind him. As incredible as her body felt, her heart hurt. She felt the bile rise in her throat.

She hated him. He was a sleazy bastard. She couldn't wait to get away from him.

Rising from the bed, Cori went into the small bath-room. It was decorated for a woman—the walls were covered in a textured, cream-colored wallpaper, and the area rug under her feet was soft and a beautiful shade of mulberry. The hand towels and soap dispenser coordinated perfectly. Under the counter, she found clean towels, toothbrushes, and a box of tampons.

Trying not to think of how many women had used this bathroom before her, she shimmied out of her clothes and stepped under the spray of cold water. Quickly, she washed and dried herself.

She loathed the idea of wearing something that had belonged to one of his conquests, but she realized she hated the idea of putting her soiled clothes back on even more.

Taking a breath, she worried what type of lacey bits of nothing she would find inside the dresser. After opening the drawer slowly, she was pleasantly surprised. Inside were flannel pants, sweatpants, and t-shirts. Nothing skimpy or sleazy at all. Since there was no way she was putting on anyone's underwear, she didn't bother looking for them and opted for going bare.

She pulled out a fluffy pair of sweatpants and a blue shirt to match. The cotton fabric felt soft on her skin and smelled freshly laundered. She crawled under the covers, enjoying the cool feeling of the sheets on her bare toes. She could hear Paxton talking to someone down the hall, but he wasn't loud enough for her to make out what he was saying. Pulling the covers up over her head, she prayed that sleep would find her soon.

After a restless night, Cori crawled out of bed with the sun. She wanted to get away from Paxton as soon as she could. She'd replayed last night's events in her head a hundred times and still couldn't believe she let him play her the way he did. And the worst part? She liked it. For that, she hated herself. She needed to stay far away from the sexy giant.

Hustling downstairs, she found Paxton stretched out on the couch with a cup of coffee, his bare, muscular chest mocking her. *Couldn't he put on a shirt?*

He flashed her a grin. "Sleep well?"

She ignored what he was implying. "Thank you for helping me last night with the police. I'm sorry I imposed. I'll get out of your hair now."

She turned on her heel and made a beeline for the front door, swiping her keys off the table as she passed it. She was halfway across her yard before she looked back. That was a huge mistake.

He stood on his front porch, his arms folded over his massive chest, watching her scurry away like a scared little mouse. She didn't need what he was offering. She wasn't going to be a part of his harem. But god, he looked good. She focused on getting back home without another look back.

Once she was inside, Cori took a shower in the guest bathroom. She would wash the clothes she'd borrowed and return them to Paxton as soon as possible. While the clothes were washing, Cori sat down at her laptop and opened her email. There were dozens of unread messages. Half of them were from Luke Williams, the widower of Rebecca. He had a lot of horrible things to say to her. Could he be the person doing these things? To what end?

After reading the fifth email out of eleven from him, Cori couldn't stomach anymore and yet she couldn't stop reading the words on the screen. This was worse than the grieving rantings of a man who'd lost his wife. His words chilled her to the bone. *"Did you like my gift? Don't worry, there's more to come. I'm just getting started."* Was he admitting to the flowers? The poor animal that had suffered horribly? Perhaps both. She closed her laptop. She had a bedroom to sterilize.

SEVEN
LUKE

LUKE WAS CONCEALED a few houses down as he watched the police officers swarming around Cori's place. Something looked off about her as she exited the man's house. She seemed...guarded. That wasn't the effect he was going for. He wanted her afraid, but she didn't look scared. *Damn it.*

He wanted to pace the patch of grass surrounding him, but even at night dressed in black, he would be easily discovered. Then he noticed a sky-blue Volvo parked just a few feet away, its occupant still inside.

He gritted his teeth—was it an undercover officer? Had he been spotted? That wouldn't be good. No, not at all. Things were not going as planned, and that was unacceptable. He turned his attention back to Cori. She was going back inside again. There was nothing more he could do with all the cops hanging around.

He carefully made his way back to his car at the end of the street. The engine came to life just as the blue Volvo came to a stop at the stop sign.

Luke decided to follow it. The car pulled into a motel

not far from Cori's house. Luke would've described the man driving as the "nerdy" type. He wore a pair of tan slacks and a green polo shirt. Luke couldn't tell what type of shoes he was wearing, but they looked like soft brown leather.

Once the stranger entered the room, Luke got out of his car. He did his best to try to peek through the curtains without looking like he was. He couldn't see anything through the sliver where they separated.

He walked back to where his car was and leaned against the hood. As if fate were on his side, the man came out of his room with a small plastic bucket. He walked toward the ice machine, leaving the door propped open slightly. Luke felt the smile spread on his face as he quickly entered the room.

He whistled once he crossed the threshold. There were pictures of Cori all over the place: in frames by the bed, stuck to the mirrors, and taped on the walls. Most looked like she was dressed for the office, but there were a bunch taken recently. In the background of one of the photos, Luke spotted himself. *Shit.* He kept looking and found himself or his car in at least a half dozen photos.

Panicked, he started tearing them down.

A soft, confused voice startled him. "W-What are you doing in my room?"

Luke spun around. He was face to face with the Volvo owner. The man started toward the door. "I'm getting the manager!" he called over his shoulder.

Luke couldn't allow that. He grabbed a lamp off the table and hit the guy in the head. The man crumbled to the floor.

Luke shut the room's door and turned back to the man, who was now crying and cradling his bloodied forehead.

He couldn't be allowed to tell anyone. Luke swung the lamp again. And again. And again, until the man lay there in a pool of blood.

Luke looked down at himself; he was covered in blood. He grabbed the bag from the trash, stripped out of his clothes, and put them inside. He rinsed himself in the shower and slipped into clothes from the dead man's suitcase. The pants were a little big, but they would do. After that, he removed all the pictures, adding them to the bag with his clothes. He couldn't justify wasting a paid room, so he lay down on the bed and decided to catch a few hours of sleep.

EIGHT
TANK

PAXTON WATCHED Cori practically run from his house. He wasn't sure why that bothered him, but it did. That was just one more reason to keep away from her. He was a complications free kind of man, and she was nothing if not complicated. But damn, if she didn't have an ass he wouldn't mind seeing bent over the side of his bed.

He made sure she got into the house without any trouble, then returned to his spot on the couch. He was tired after tossing and turning all night. Knowing she was just across the hall all night made sleeping almost impossible. He couldn't help but replay the night's events in his mind over and over. He closed his eyes now and it all came back to him again. Her smell, her taste, her touch. It was all intoxicating.

He lay there trying not to think of her. He needed some rest. He wasn't sure how long he had been asleep before the bang of his screen door woke him.

"You're lucky I'm not an intruder," a low, female voice said.

"You *are* an intruder," he grumbled.

Krysta smiled from ear to ear. "Is that any way to talk to your favorite sister?"

"You're my only sister, thank God. I couldn't deal with more than one of you. Hell, I can barely deal with one." But he smiled.

"I love you too."

He pushed himself up into a sitting position. "So what brings you to town this time?"

"Just needed to get away for a bit. Clear my head. I'll stay out of your way." Krysta made a cross motion over her heart. "Cross my heart."

Paxton jumped up off the couch and swung Krysta into a big bear hug. He liked having her there; he missed her when she wasn't around, though he'd never admit that to her. Plus, he could look out for her when she was with him. She lived almost two hours away, and he wished like hell that she'd move back.

Krysta giggled. "Let me down. I'm not a kid anymore."

"You'll always be my kid sister."

She was right, though. She wasn't a little kid anymore. At twenty-five, she was a beautiful woman. Long chestnut hair cascaded halfway down her back. She was tall for a woman, just an inch or two shy of six feet, and slender. She was a graphic designer, so as long as she had her laptop she could work from anywhere—she frequently used Paxton's kitchen table.

"Gag," she teased. "I'm gonna grab a quick shower."

"Oh shit, let me clean it for you real quick."

Krysta wrinkled her nose. "Someone used it?"

"My neighbor had a problem last night and needed a place to stay."

She eyed him suspiciously. "Paxton, what are you getting yourself in to?"

He kissed her forehead. "Nothing. I promise." He smiled down at her.

"Ahem." An unexpected voice sounded from just outside.

They both turned to the open front door. Cori stood on the other side of the screen with a pair of sweats folded in her arm. His gaze swept over her body. Her tank top and cut-off shorts showcased her curves—Paxton felt his cock take notice too. Then he got to her face. She looked pissed off and he had a pretty good idea what she was thinking. This wasn't good.

"Oh, hey. I'm Krysta." His sister looked back and forth between him and Cori.

"Looks like you'll be needing these again." Cori thrust the clothing at him before stomping off his porch like a toddler.

Krysta turned to look him in the eye. "Oh, big brother. What did you do? Tell me you didn't have sex with that girl?"

"I can honestly say, I didn't."

"You might wanna talk to her." She eyed the bundle in his hand. "Are those mine?"

Paxton handed the clothes to her. "Yeah, sorry. I'll be back."

He marched out of the house like a man on a mission. He tried Cori's front door—it was locked. *Good girl.* He knocked loudly. After the third knock, Paxton headed around the back. He could see her sitting at the kitchen table, staring blankly at it. He tapped on the glass. Cori looked up at him with her lips curled in disgust.

"Open this damn door, Cori."

She responded by giving him the middle finger. Anger boiled inside of him. He should just say screw it and walk away. If it were any other fucking woman on the planet, he would. But for some unknown reason, what she thought of him mattered. He didn't like it one bit.

He knocked harder with the side of his fist. She gave him both fingers this time.

"I'm not playin', babe. Open this door or I'll make sure every neighbor can hear what I need to say to you and I'll do it nude on your front porch."

She dashed to the door. After flipping the latch, she opened it. "You're an asshole," she pouted.

"Yup."

"What do you want now? I'm busy."

He made it a point to look around the room. "Busy doing what? Seething?"

"I don't know what the hell you're talking about."

"Could you have been any ruder to Krysta?"

"I'm surprised you can keep all their names straight."

He took both of her arms in his hands, rendering her upper body immobile. Her stunned silence gave him the opportunity to speak uninterrupted.

"Now listen to me. That's the third time you've insulted my character. Personally, it is what it is. I'm not a choir boy—I don't claim to be, either. However, at some point, you're going to apologize to Krysta."

"The hell I will," she yelled back in his face.

With her back now pressed up against the kitchen wall, he was able to let go of one of her arms. He took ahold of her chin and gazed into her eyes. There was a fire raging behind them. He wanted to play with it.

"If she were just some chick, I wouldn't care. But no one treats my kid sister like shit when I'm around. Understood?"

The color drained from her face. "Your sister?"

"You stayed in her room last night."

"Oh my god." Her eyes closed slowly, and her head tipped back until it hit the wall.

Her neck was now on display, and the skin looked soft and smooth. He wanted to run his tongue across her pulse there. He wanted to taste it. He needed to keep his wits about him, he reminded himself.

Her eyes opened. They locked gazes. She moistened her lips. That peek of her tongue was his undoing.

His lips crashed down on hers. He entwined their fingers before holding them up above her head. Her breasts were thrust forward with the motion, and they pressed against him invitingly. He promised himself he would get acquainted with them soon. Real soon.

Their tongues dueled. Cori tried to get her hands free, but he wasn't having that. He liked having her under his control. The minx took a bite of his lower lip, and blood rushed to his cock in record time. She was feisty. He liked that.

He let her arms fall so he could work the button on her shorts. She clamped her small hands over his, and he recognized it for the rejection it was. Paxton stepped away.

Cori was breathing heavily, her chest rising and falling in a way that only turned him on more. Unfortunately, he couldn't ignore her "no."

But she advanced, surprising him, and took his hand in hers. She looked up at him shyly. "Maybe we should take this upstairs?"

———

CORI

Cori couldn't believe she had just asked him that. Not after what he did to her last night. Maybe it was *because* of what he did last night. Her body craved him. She needed what he had to offer her, even if it was only once. She needed to feel wanted again. The faster they got upstairs, the faster they could get naked.

"Sure, babe. I could carry you upstairs. Lay you down softly on a bed and give you what you want." He grinned knowingly at her. "Or...I could pull off those cute shorts, spin you around, and fuck you against this wall, giving you what you need. The choice is yours."

She was speechless. She felt naughty just entertaining the notion of having sex, not only in the kitchen, but in broad daylight, no less. Her eyes searched his, which were full of mischief.

He was too far from her. She missed his touch. She missed his kiss. Without allowing herself another moment to think, Cori pulled her shirt over her head. The air chilled her overheated skin. Her nipples hardened against the silky material of her bra.

She felt exposed. Paxton watched her with hungry eyes. Her skin tingled wherever his gaze landed. Swallowing hard, she reached behind her back, unclasping her bra. She let the straps slide down her arms and the bra drop to the floor. Paxton's tongue traced his bottom lip. Slowly. She wanted to taste his lip herself.

Stepping forward, she placed her hand on his chest. Paxton didn't move. His intense stare burned into her. Reaching behind his neck, she gently pulled him toward her as she went up on her tiptoes. She searched his eyes one last time before she pressed her lips to his.

His large hands gripped her hips, lifting her feet right off the ground. She wrapped her legs around his waist, latching her ankles together for better hold.

Her naked back hit the cool plaster of the kitchen wall. Her senses were overwhelmed. The cool at her back, the heat of his body in front of her. The clock ticked loudly on the wall next to her head…counting the seconds until this man gave her what she desperately needed.

Paxton broke off their kiss. "You know this isn't a good idea. Right?"

"I know."

"It won't end well."

"I don't care."

Even as the words left her mouth, she knew they were lies. She *would* care. She had never been one for casual sex and Paxton was the type of man that didn't do commitment—that was painstakingly obvious. She wasn't going to let that stop her, though. Not this time. He pulled her away from the wall, laying her on the kitchen table. Cori was surprised her panties didn't melt off from the way he was looking at her. She could only describe it as primal desire.

This time he unzipped her shorts slowly. Keeping his eyes locked with hers, he pulled on the fabric. She lifted her hips as best as she could with her legs dangling over the side of the table. Once her shorts and panties dropped to the floor, Paxton took his eyes off hers. He gazed down at her bare mound.

"Fucking beautiful," he whispered. "Just like I knew you would be."

Paxton got down on his knees, running his fingertips tenderly up her thighs. Gooseflesh broke out across her skin. She could feel his breath before his lips touched her.

She lifted her head to be able to see him. His eyes gleamed with eagerness. The moment had arrived. He pressed his lips against her opening. He began kissing her, and his tongue swept from bottom to top before he spread her lips open with his fingers.

He sucked her clit into his mouth and that was her undoing. Her head fell back, creating a loud thud on the table. He stopped for a moment, only to attack her with more fervor. Her breath quickened in time to the orgasm building inside of her. Her hands gripped the edges of the table as she skyrocketed to her climax. Paxton kept licking and sucking until all her bones had melted.

He stood up and produced his wallet, where he'd hidden a foil wrapper. Cori watched from the table top, her shaking arms barely propping her up for a better view. Her legs were still dangling. She'd never been one of those girls that went nuts over a guy with ink, but holy hell, she was when that ink was branded on *him*. Every movement caused his tattoos to ripple, highlighting the toned muscle underneath.

Putting the condom between his teeth, he began unbuttoning his pants. He pushed them down his unbelievably thick thighs. Muscles bunched and moved with an animalistic beauty as he pulled them off completely.

Oh sweet baby Jesus. She wasn't mistaken when she'd seen him naked in his living room. She was staring. She knew she was, but seriously, how could she not? How the hell was that going to fit inside her? He tore open the packet, then rolled it down his cock. A knowing smile spread across his face. Heat blossomed on her cheeks. He leaned over her, kissing her breathless yet again.

"Last chance, sweetheart," he whispered against her neck.

Touching the side of his face, she waited until he looked up at her. "I want this," she sighed.

Paxton wrapped his arms behind her until his hands were over her shoulders. She felt trapped, only in the best way. His kiss was calm and gentle. He pushed up against her entrance. Her body teetered on pleasure and pain as he slowly entered her. Each inch stretched her in a way she had never felt before. Once he was as deep as he could get, he paused. Concern was written across his handsome face.

"Am I hurting you?"

She shook her head from side to side. "Don't fuckin' stop."

An impish grin adorned his face. "Your wish is my command."

Paxton started with long, slow strokes. The kitchen faded into the background. All she could see was his face above her. All she could hear were the soft grunts with each plunge he took. Her body was overloaded with all things Paxton. He smelled like soap, sweat, and sex. It was an intoxicating mixture.

"That's it, sweetheart. Just let go."

She was close. So very close. Her moans filled the room as she drove her hips up to meet his. Over and over again.

"Paxton!" a female voice shouted in disbelief.

In shock, Cori tried to get up. However, she was still locked in his arms. Embarrassment flooded her.

"Krysta, I love you, but go the fuck home," he barked.

Cori tried to get up. She couldn't believe his sister was standing at her back door looking through the window. Forget embarrassed—she was mortified. But she couldn't move.

He focused his attention back to Cori. "Where the hell do you think you're trying to go?"

"Your sister—"

"Can watch for all I care." He laughed. "We're not done until you're screaming my name and that sweet pussy milks my cock dry. Now hold on tight."

Cori threw her arms around his neck. Knowing that nothing was going to stop him from having her only turned her on more. He increased his speed and strength until he plunged into her like a piston. Her body instantly reacted. Just as he predicted, she screamed out his name. Cori came with such force, her entire body seized up.

"Mmmmm," he sighed. "Good girl."

He stood up to his full height and dragged her closer to the edge of the table. She thought for sure she would fall off, the way her ass hung over the side. He slipped back inside, taking what he needed. His face was slightly contorted in pleasure and Cori felt a primitive sense of pride. He was beautiful. And in that moment, he was hers. Knowing it would soon end felt like a weight over her heart.

His loud groan brought her back into the here and now. She could feel him swell the instant before he erupted inside of her. He reminded her of a caged animal bursting free from its captor. It was like nothing she had ever heard or felt before. He draped himself across her and held her in a vise grip. It was empowering. She held onto him, her fingertips digging into his shoulders. She didn't want this moment to end.

He raised his head, gazing into her eyes. There was something in them that she couldn't describe. "That was intense."

Cori just nodded in agreement. She was afraid of what her stupid mouth might say if she opened it. He kissed her sweetly before withdrawing. He strolled to the trashcan in all his glory. After disposing of the condom, he picked up his pants. She watched him dress without moving.

"I gotta run. I need to see what Krysta needed so badly that she had to walk over here."

"Sure."

Without a backward glance, he ambled out of the same door he'd entered. Did he know he had taken her heart with him?

NINE
TANK

LEAVING Cori spread out naked on her kitchen table was the worst thing he could have possibly done. He knew that. He knew she was probably cursing him already and he hadn't even made it to his house yet. He felt like a piece of shit, but he had to go. Something happened back there. Something he couldn't describe. Or maybe it was something he *wouldn't* describe. Either way, he needed time alone to think. Krysta was the perfect excuse to high-tail it out of there.

There she waited, inside the door with her hands on her hips like their mother used to do when they came home after curfew. All Krysta needed was an oversized nightgown and robe.

She glowered at him. "Thought you said you weren't sleeping with the cute neighbor girl?"

"Did you see either of us sleeping?" He chuckled, trying to play it off.

"Don't do that." She held up her hand in a stop gesture. "You know what I mean. You're playing with fire this time, Paxton."

"What's that supposed to mean?"

"This isn't going to end well."

"Mind your own, little sister."

Paxton moved past her. She was right, of course. It wouldn't end well. He should have, at the very least, helped her up. *Shit.* He was such an ass. Pissed at himself, he plopped down on the couch. Krysta turned to scowl at him.

"Not every girl is Gillian."

Paxton shot up from the couch. "Don't even say her name in this house."

He escaped to the kitchen, retrieving a bottle of water from the stainless-steel fridge. He had just cracked the seal when Krysta came around the corner.

"She wasn't the one, Paxton. She didn't deserve you. I told you that from the beginning."

"Look—"

"No, *you* look," she interrupted. "There's a woman out there for you. Not that you'll ever know if you keep burning through them the way you have been."

"I'm not ready."

"Not all relationships are shit. Remember, you had some good times."

"Of course, I remember. Then life happens. I worked too much and she played too much. Now, I end it before it goes to shit."

"I call bullshit."

Paxton glared at her. "You can call whatever you want. I don't see you settling down with anyone?"

"Actually…" She paused, looking at him for a moment. "Bentley proposed last week."

"What?" he barked. "You've only been seeing him a few months."

"So? He's a nice guy. He comes from a good family."

"He's a trust fund baby and his father is a politician. Do you love him? Did you accept? Why the fuck am I just hearing about this now?"

"I told him I had to get away for a few days and think about it. I don't know if I love him. Like you said, we haven't been seeing each other long."

"Well, I know one thing," he said smugly.

"What's that, all-knowing Oz?"

"There's no way you love him. You wouldn't have to think about it. You'd know." Realization dawned on him. "So that's why you're here now? Contemplating a proposal from a man you don't love? That doesn't sound like you."

"You wouldn't understand."

"Try me."

"Please. Can we drop it for now?"

Paxton took her into his arms. He wanted to push her for answers, but he knew if he did, she would push back for answers as well. So he let go for now. "Sure, kid."

He kissed her forehead. He hated fighting with Krysta; she meant the world to him. He didn't want to argue with her anymore. "I'm sorry I yelled."

The squeal of tires caught both of their attention. A bad feeling settled in his gut as he ran out the front door. A dark sedan sped down the otherwise silent street. Cori was looking out of her window while talking on the phone.

She disappeared for a moment before opening the front door.

"What the hell was that all about?" he yelled from his front porch.

She crossed her arms over her chest in defiance. "Some creep. This neighborhood seems full of them."

He didn't miss the dig she tossed at him. He wasn't about to address it now though. Not with Krysta standing behind him. He took off toward Cori's house. After stomping up the steps, he stopped in front of her, mimicking her stance.

"What was said creeper doing?"

"He was peeping in my window."

"Hmmm," he replied thoughtfully, "you're right. There seems to be a lot of that around here lately."

Crimson blossomed across Cori's cheeks. It was possibly the cutest thing he had ever seen. He'd caused his fair share of women to blush, but with Cori, the blush covered her entire face and even her ears turned red. It was so damn cute, he wanted to pull her close and taste her lips.

"Anyway," she deflected. "He had on a mask. I couldn't see any features except that he was white and had brown eyes."

"Who were you talking to?"

"I called Detective Hyland as soon as I saw him."

"Good. I'm going to run to the office, see if Mother has anything. Maybe you should come with me?"

She cocked an eyebrow. "Why would I do that?"

"I'm not leaving you alone while I'm gone."

Krysta giggled behind him. He threw a dirty look over his shoulder at her.

"He's gone now. I'm not going anywhere with you."

"You stubborn woman."

"And you're a dick."

"Hey guys?" Krysta interjected. He turned to face his sister yet again. "How about I hang with Cori and you go do whatever it is you gotta do."

Paxton thought about it for a moment. Krysta was well

versed in self-defense. He'd made sure she was trained properly years ago. If Cori stayed with her, that would work too. He looked back and forth between the two women.

"Do you have your Ruger?"

"Yes, Dad," she replied sarcastically. She really was a pain in the ass. Both of them were, he realized.

"Shut up, Krysta."

"You told me to always keep it with me, and I do. We'll be fine here."

He pinned Cori with his glare. "Is that acceptable, sweetheart?"

"Don't 'sweetheart' me."

She looked like she was one snarky comment away from stomping her feet. He tried not to laugh.

"Ms. Transue, will you please keep my little sister company, in the safety of my home, while I'm gone?"

"I hate you," she replied.

Placing his hands above his head on the door frame, he leaned into her. His mouth pressed up against the shell of her ear. He whispered so Krysta couldn't hear him, "Not even a little."

Righting himself, he left her standing in the doorway, mouth agape. He was halfway to his truck before he heard her yell.

"Considerably!"

———

CORI

"Is he always this bossy?"

"No." Krysta grinned. "He's usually much worse."

"Oh god."

Krysta laughed as she started walking toward the house. "It's not so bad. Come on over." She waggled her eyebrows. "I'll tell you all the dirty little secrets my big, bad ass brother has."

No way was Cori going to pass up information on her grumpy neighbor. She grabbed her keys and purse off the table. She made sure the door locked behind her and she followed Krysta to Paxton's house. Once they were inside, Krysta plopped down in a leather recliner. She reclined back until her feet were almost level with her head.

She hadn't realized the family resemblance at first. Then again, she wasn't thinking clearly the first time she saw them together. They had the same eyes. Krysta had beautiful long hair. She was slender and carried herself like a strong, confident woman.

"What do you wanna know?" She grinned mischievously. That smile was definitely familiar.

"So, what's his problem?"

"Oh, honey, you're gonna need to be more specific."

"He's…well, grumpy. And bossy, and aggravating."

Krysta laughed. "So how long have you had the hots for my brother?"

Cori shrugged her shoulders. "I don't."

Krysta smiled. "Yeah, okay."

She didn't want the conversation to wrap around to herself. She wanted to know about Paxton. What type of man was he, really? What made him tick? Most importantly, what could she do to ensure he was thinking about her, as much as she couldn't stop thinking about him?

"He used to be a cop, didn't he?" she asked.

Krysta nodded. "Tank was a great cop. Even if he was a

workaholic. Then again, maybe that's why he was so great."

"Then why isn't he anymore?"

"He was shot in the line of duty. The bastard that shot him took his knee out. Does he look like a desk jockey to you?"

Cori thought back to Paxton kicking her door in. She pictured the determination that was evident in every step he took up to her front door after the flowers appeared. No, he wasn't a man who sat around watching things happen. He was a take-action type of man.

"No. I can't imagine that."

"It was really hard on him. Him and Max. They were after this guy who abducted a child. They were so close. They got a tip and tracked him down. Unfortunately, the guy was armed. As Tank took chase, he was hit. Max refused to leave him. They lost the guy. To this day it's an open case. Look," Krysta continued, "if you really like my brother the way I think you do, don't give up on him."

"I don't know him well enough to—"

"Please, don't insult my intelligence. Kitchen table aside, I saw the way you looked at him when you didn't know who I was. I'm a woman too. I know that look."

Cori's cheeks heated. "I'm so embarrassed about what you witnessed."

"Number one, *I* was the one peeking in *your* window. I should be the embarrassed one. Number two, that shit is seriously hot...you know, if my brother wasn't involved." She scrunched her nose in disgust. Cori laughed.

"I'm serious, Cori. My brother is emotionally challenged. If you want him, you're gonna have to work for him."

"I don't know how long I'm going to stay in town."

Krysta crossed her arms. "You bought a house here. Try again."

"In light of the current situation, I—"

"Bullshit. Third time is a charm, go ahead."

Cori looked down at her hands. She twisted them in her lap for a moment before she looked up again. "I'm afraid he could break me."

Krysta nodded as if in agreement. She sat up straight in the chair. "Now that's a real answer. One I can sympathize with."

"Have you ever unknowingly given your heart to a man that's unattainable?"

Sadness washed over her beautiful face. Cori watched as the scene played out in Krysta's mind. It was evident that whatever she was remembering filled her with both love and remorse. "Every day, Cori. Every. Damn. Day."

"How do you do it?"

"I don't. We aren't together. That's why I'm the perfect person to tell you: Don't give up."

Cori wasn't sure what broke her heart more, the sadness in Krysta's eyes or the knowledge that someday her own eyes would tell a story of sorrow. What happened, happened. The only way to save her heart was to make sure it was a one and done situation. She placed her hand over her stomach, hoping to staunch the ache she felt.

"What time do you think he'll be back?"

Krysta shrugged her shoulders. "Never know with him. Wanna watch a movie to pass time?"

"Sure."

Krysta put in a DVD and next thing Cori knew, she was waking up on Paxton's couch. She didn't know how long she had been asleep. It was dark out and Krysta was arguing with someone at the front door.

"I said he's not here. Go home."

A female voice answered her. "I know what you said, Krysta. I said I want to come in and wait for him."

"No." The vehemence in her voice surprised Cori.

"I need to talk to him."

"You don't need to do anything, except move your ass off this porch."

Cori approached the door. "Everything okay?"

"It will be."

"Who's that?" the mystery woman questioned.

Cori kept moving toward the front door until she came face to face with a beautiful redhead. She had legs that seemed to go on forever and a dress that did nothing to hide them. The white of the dress contrasted beautifully with her tanned flesh. She looked at Cori as if she had left a bad taste in her mouth.

"None of your business, Gillian. Now go home before I shoot you for trespassing."

"Tell Tank to call me."

"What makes you think he ever wants to speak to *you* again?"

The woman, Gillian, sneered at them. "He promised he'd never love anyone like he loved me."

"That was almost two years ago. Move on—he has."

"Is that a fact?" Gillian scoffed.

Krysta practically growled at the woman, "Yes."

"We'll just have to see about that."

The woman spun around on her spiky heels so quickly, Cori was certain she'd fall. She stomped down the porch stairs. Somehow she managed to gracefully fold herself into the tiny red sports car she was driving. What a cliché. Krysta slammed the door before turning to face Cori.

Krysta looked pissed off. "Sorry about that."

"Who was she?"

"Paxton's past."

A woman he slept with? No, she said *love*. She had to have been more important than a hookup. She must be the last serious relationship he'd had. Would Krysta volunteer any more information? After a few minutes of silence, Cori thought better of asking. Resuming her spot on the couch, Cori used her phone to pull up her email. She spent the next half hour responding to a dozen emails from friends and colleagues.

Multiple car doors opening jolted her from her reading. Krysta was up in a flash, looking out the window.

"Great, just what we need."

Cori was about to ask her what she meant when Paxton barged through the front door. He was laughing and talking to someone Cori couldn't see yet. Damn, she loved his laugh. It was husky and sent shivers down her spine. Her entire body became aware when he entered the room. He glanced in her direction, grinning. The butterflies in her stomach must have been what were holding her upright because her knees were definitely weak.

"...so then this bitch—" The man stopped mid-sentence. "Hey, Krysta. I didn't know you were in town."

"I didn't realize I had to ask your permission."

"Guys," Paxton warned.

The guy smirked at Cori. He had blond hair that came down to his chin, and tattoos covering both of his arms. He looked like the type of bad boy her sister, Brianna, would drool over. "Well, well. You must be the Doc."

"I don't know if I must be, but I am."

"We haven't properly been introduced. I'm this big lug's best friend, Kasper. Affectionately known as Gutter Mouth."

"Ahh…now I remember."

"See, unforgettable. That's me."

Cori shook her head while laughing. Krysta walked in between the two of them. "I don't know if I'd go that far."

"Krysta, honey, you couldn't forget me if you tried." Kasper winked at Paxton's sister.

"You won't stay gone long enough to give me the chance." Krysta turned to Cori. "It was nice hanging out with you. I'm gonna go crash."

"You too. Thank you."

Krysta started walking toward the hallway that lead to the bedrooms. Stopping short, she turned slowly. "Cori," she called back.

"Yeah?"

"Remember what I said."

Out of the corner of her eye, Cori spotted Paxton's confused scowl. "What did she say?" he asked.

Cori's gaze drifted back to Krysta's. She couldn't risk making eye contact with Paxton now. He might see her for the liar she was. "Nothing important."

Krysta gave her a sad nod, an acknowledgement of the unspoken agreement they now had. Cori watched Krysta's back until she disappeared down the hall. Her skin began to crawl. Chancing a look in Paxton's direction, she found both men glaring at her. *Uh oh.* This could get awkward.

Paxton shoved his hands into his front pockets. "What the hell was that all about?"

"Nothing."

"Didn't seem like it was nothing," he growled.

She put her hands on her hips. She was annoyed with his macho bullshit. "Can I go home now?"

"She's feisty. I like her." Kasper guffawed.

Paxton scowled at her. "You're exhausting."

"I'm taking that as a yes." Cori turned to Kasper. "It was nice meeting you."

After retrieving her phone from the arm of the couch, she made her way to the front door. She was stepping onto the porch when Paxton grabbed ahold of her arm, stopping her from getting any farther. He looked like he had a dozen things to say to her; she didn't want to hear them. She wanted her life back. Life pre-Paxton.

"We need to talk."

She kept her eyes trained on his throat. She wasn't going to meet his eyes. "No, we don't."

"Cori, don't."

"We have nothing to talk about." She tried to wrench her arm free from his grasp. Paxton wasn't having it. She didn't want to hurt him, but she didn't want him to hurt *her*, either. Fortifying her stand, she looked up into his eyes. "Gillian, however, would *love* for you to call her. Insisted, actually."

Paxton released her as if she'd burned him. She stumbled backward. The softness in his eyes hardened. She could see the vein in his neck pulse. At that moment, he was scary.

He gritted his teeth. "Goodbye, Cori."

Paxton slammed the heavy wooden door in her face, narrowly missing her nose. She felt like absolute shit, but she accomplished her goal. Her sexy neighbor would no longer bother her. She could get back to her life. She just had to find out who was watching her now and all would be right in the world.

She walked back to her house slowly. That's when she remembered she still needed a new mattress. *Ugh*. She sure as hell couldn't ask Paxton for help now. She closed the door behind her and plopped down on the couch. Looking out of the side window, she could see Paxton and Kasper talking. Paxton's hands were waving all over the place.

She couldn't stand watching him now. Not after knowing how much she'd pissed him off. She should have put blinds on all the windows in the house. She lay down on the couch so she could no longer see out of the window. Her last thought before falling asleep was that she needed to disinfect her kitchen table before she ate on it.

———

TANK

The fury he felt over hearing that bitch's name from Cori's sweet lips pushed him over the edge. He was seething inside. When the hell had Gillian been here? Only two people knew the answer to that question, and he'd just slammed the door in one of their faces.

Gutter Mouth held his hand up. "Dude, chill. You're gonna pop a vein."

"She was here," Paxton murmured as he paced the room. "She was fucking *here*."

"I heard. When's the last time you talked to her?"

"When I was packing my things."

Gutter Mouth whistled. "Wow. Are you gonna call her?"

Paxton looked at his best friend with what he could only assume was a look of disgust. That's certainly what he felt. Gillian was in a past he didn't want to relive. Ever.

"Are you nuts?" Paxton continued to pace his living room. He had too much anger to sit still. He hollered up the steps for his sister. "Krysta!"

"What are you doing, Tank?"

He scowled at Gutter Mouth. "Getting answers."

"Oh boy."

They could hear Krysta clomp down the stairs. She was running her fingers through her long hair.

"What the hell?" she snarled.

"She was here? What did she say?"

"Oh shit. How did...Cori? Look, I told her to get lost."

"What did she want?"

"You, big brother. She wants you."

"Shit," he thundered.

"She came here dressed like slutty Barbie in her flashy sports car."

"How did Cori react?"

"She was surprised to see her, but she didn't say anything about it after the bitch left. I was a little surprised she didn't ask, to be honest."

Paxton ran his hands across his head. The prickly hairs scratched against his palms. This was the last thing he needed. Why now? What could she want with him now?

Krysta looked around the room. "Where's Cori?"

"Mr. Charisma threw her out after she said a certain name." Gutter Mouth rolled his eyes.

"You what?" Krysta blurted out furiously.

"She was already leaving. I didn't throw her out." Paxton threw his best friend a dirty look. "Gutter Mouth, you're an asshole."

"No, dude. You didn't throw her out, you just slammed the door in her pretty little face."

"Paxton, no. Please tell me he's exaggerating like

usual." His sister pleaded for him to tell her his big-mouthed friend was lying.

"Well…" He trailed off.

"Oh my god. What the hell is wrong with you? She really likes you. Well, that's probably past tense now," she scoffed.

That surprised him. There was a difference between liking someone and lusting after them. He was more inclined to lust. At least that's the way it had been for the last two years. Unfortunately, this time was different. He liked her too, which was why he needed to stay away from her. He wasn't the settling down type. Not anymore.

"That's not my problem." Shit. He felt like an asshole saying that. From the expression on Krysta's face, she wholeheartedly agreed. It was a mixture of disbelief and disgust.

"Could you be more of an ass fuck?"

"Yeah, actually, I think I could."

Gutter Mouth chuckled from the couch. Krysta spun on him like a woman possessed. He even leaned back into the couch to avoid the finger she was waving madly in his face.

"No one fucking asked you. You're just as bad, if not worse, than him."

"Krysta—"

"Don't 'Krysta' me. The both of you disgust me. However, you, Paxton Sokolofski. You break my heart. You don't even love yourself enough to let the anger go. All it is, is poison. So it didn't work out with Gillian. Relation-ships end. It sucks, but it happens."

"I love you, doesn't that count?" He smiled.

"And I love you. I always will. Will that be enough when you're alone at night? When you're too old to pick up that night's bed warmer?" She shook her head sadly at him. "It wouldn't be enough for me."

"Some people are meant to settle down, some aren't."

"Bullshit." Krysta stared daggers at him. "I can't even stand to look at you anymore."

She marched toward the front door.

"Where are you going?"

"Not that it's any of your business, but I'm going to Cori's."

Paxton watched his extremely pissed off little sister storm out of his house. God help the man who married her. If she married that guy, their visits would be fewer and further in between. If she visited at all. When she *did* visit, he would probably come with her. He didn't like the thought of that at all. Gutter Mouth joined him by the window.

"She's pissed, dude."

"No shit."

"So...*do* you have a thing for the Doc over there or what?"

"No."

Gutter Mouth chuckled. "That's the answer you're going with?"

"What's that supposed to mean?" Paxton glared at his best friend.

"Oh nothing. Just that, that's exactly what Max said about Sloane."

"Fuck you."

"That's what I thought."

Paxton stretched his arms up over his head. "Let's go out," he blurted, dropping them to his side.

Gutter Mouth raised a questioning eyebrow. "Yeah? Do you really think that's a good idea?"

Without answering, Paxton grabbed his wallet and keys off the table. Gutter Mouth shrugged his shoulders before heading out the front door ahead of him. Paxton locked the door. Krysta had her own key to get back in. Stepping up into his truck, Paxton quickly started it up and pulled out of his driveway.

The drive there was mostly silent. He kept visualizing the look on Cori's face when he told her goodbye. The sadness in her eyes could have been his imagination. Or was Krysta right? More importantly, was Gutter Mouth? No, he couldn't be. He didn't have anything except a brief infatuation for the raven-haired beauty next door. It would pass. It had to. Resolve in place, Paxton continued to the local watering hole. He would find a cutie to spend the night with and his sexy neighbor would be a memory before the night was over.

"Over there." Gutter Mouth nodded his head toward the end of the bar. Two woman sat giggling together. They seemed like they were alone. The blonde was pretty enough. The brunette reminded him of a certain someone he didn't want to think about.

"Let's go introduce ourselves," he urged.

As they approached the women, the blonde smiled at him. She wore too much makeup around her amber eyes, but he didn't care. She was skinny too. He would have to go easy on her, but he'd have to put forth less effort than he thought. He smiled back at her.

"Hello, ladies." Gutter Mouth's voice was as smooth as honey.

"Hello there, handsome." The brunette adjusted her posture, inviting her breasts to the conversation. Paxton wanted to laugh. He kept his face straight, for both of their sakes. Paxton stood next to the blonde's chair. She batted her fake eyelashes up at him.

"Hey there. I'm Maryanne."

"Tank."

She looked at her friend, giggling. "Well, Tank, care to buy a girl a drink?"

"Sure."

He called the bartender over and ordered beers for himself and Gutter Mouth plus two Cosmos for the ladies. Tiffany, Gutter Mouth's companion for the evening, kept talking about her favorite reality shows. How Gutter Mouth continued to smile and pretend to pay attention, Paxton would never know. Maryanne was just as animated about them.

He was bored out of his mind. Paxton couldn't take it anymore. Time to get on with it. He didn't care that they had barely touched their overpriced drinks.

He grinned. "So, would you ladies like to get out of here?"

"Yes," they spoke in unison.

"I'm in the black truck out front. You can follow us in your car."

Maryanne seemed slightly annoyed. "You don't want to ride together?"

"No."

"Come on, Maryanne. It's fine," her friend whined.

Reluctantly, Maryanne followed them outside. The air cooled his skin after being inside the heated bar. Paxton was raised to be a gentleman. He made sure the women got to their car first, then pointed out his truck for them to follow. His mind wasn't in the right place tonight. He should have just stayed home. He really didn't even want to bring these women home, but this was just what he did. Ever since things had ended with Gillian, that is. The gravel crunched under their boots as they crossed the parking lot.

"I'm not sure which one is worse," Gutter Mouth sighed as he closed the truck door.

"I know."

"Maybe I'll just put Tiffany's face into the pillow," he joked.

Paxton laughed. "That still probably won't shut her up."

"Dude, I know."

He pulled his truck into the driveway. He tried not to notice that all the lights were off at Cori's and her car was missing. Where could she have gone? Was Krysta back home or were they together? Shit. He forgot Krysta was staying with him. Nothing he could do about it now.

There was a nagging feeling in the back of his head. This was a mistake.

The girls parked behind him. They giggled all the way to his front door. Paxton wondered how long it would take to get Maryanne undressed. A quick fuck and then they could both leave. Pushing the door open, he looked around for any telltale signs of Krysta being home. All was quiet. Good. He turned on only one dimmed light, casting most of the room in shadows.

"Make yourselves at home. Can I get you a drink?"

Tiffany smiled. "Whatever you're having is fine."

Paxton retrieved four bottles of beer from the fridge, once again asking himself why he was doing this. He didn't need to get laid. He'd had great sex this afternoon with Cori...there it was. He was trying to erase Cori, and Maryanne was going to help him.

Gutter Mouth and Tiffany were already making out on his recliner. He took a spot on the couch next to Maryanne.

She licked her lips slowly, silently offering him a taste. Paxton threaded his fingers in her hair, drawing her forward. It wasn't nearly as silky as Cori's. *Fuck.* This wasn't going to work if he kept thinking of her. He pressed his lips firmly to hers. She was a decent kisser at least. He could definitely work with that. Without his usual amount of foreplay, he tugged her dress up over her head. The purple bra she wore matched perfectly with her barely there panties. He could hear Tiffany moaning from the recliner.

Dragging Maryanne's bra straps down her light brown skin, he kissed his way down her neck and collarbone, burying his face in her cleavage. She smelled of jasmine. He had just taken a pert nipple between his teeth when the front door opened and the lights came on. Momentarily blinded, it took Paxton a moment to realize an extremely pissed off Krysta stood before him.

It wouldn't be the first time she'd walked in on him with a girl. However, it was the first time it happened while Gutter Mouth was there shirtless with his hand up his own date's dress. But the worst part of the whole situation was standing behind Krysta. Cori stared at him as though he'd grown horns and a long, pointy tail. Maryanne used his body to shield hers as the girls stood there.

"Okay, Max is waiting...oh my..." Sloane stopped dead in her tracks, turning her body so Mia couldn't see into the living room.

He was in hell.

Cori pushed past Sloane, fleeing from his house of debauchery.

"You son of a bitch!" Krysta spat.

Tiffany stood up with a smug look on her face. "Um, who the hell are you?"

Krysta crossed the room, standing toe to toe with Tiffany. His sister stood a good two inches taller than her. This wasn't going to end well. His baby sister was not someone to trifle with—he'd made sure of that.

Handing Maryanne her dress, he got up from where he'd been lying.

Krysta pointed in Paxton's direction. "I'm his sister." Then at Gutter Mouth. "And his wife."

"Wife!" cried Tiffany. "Maryanne, let's get outta here. Assholes."

His best buddy plopped his ass in the recliner, laughing. Paxton didn't know what was so funny. They were in serious shit. Knowing they were playboys and seeing it firsthand were two separate things. Having Sloane witness his behavior bothered him. It bothered him even more that his sweet little Mia was in her arms.

"Hey, Mia. How's my favorite girl tonight?" He took a step in their direction.

Sloane held up her hand, shaking her head at him. "Not until you wash the skank off, Paxton."

He stopped. She was right. He'd tainted every relationship he'd had in the past few years. Whether it was romantic or platonic, he always did something to fuck it up. He would never taint what he had with Mia. That was enough to get Gutter Mouth to stop with his fucking laughter too. Sloane was the only woman they really respected. He respected his sister and Mia too, but that was different.

"Anyway, the reason we're here is to help Cori," Sloane said. "She's pretty great, you know. She came by the office earlier and us girls went out to dinner. To make a long story short…"

"Too late." Gutter Mouth grinned only to receive a look of absolute destruction from Krysta.

Sloane continued without even glancing at him. "…she still needed a new mattress. I called Max and we went to pick one out. I'm here to get you guys to help move the old one out and the new one in. However, seems the circumstances are no longer ideal. Us girls will just muddle through with Max's help."

He sighed. "Sloane—"

She pinned him with a look of disappointment. "Sorry to ruin your evening."

The girls marched out of the house. He fell back onto the couch again, scrubbing his face with his hands.

"Dude, they're pissed."

"No fucking shit, Captain Obvious."

"What do we do now?"

"Now, I'm going to shower. Then I'm going over there to apologize. Hopefully then Sloane will let me hold Mia. I don't care what you do."

"Can I use your other shower? I've got a spare set of clothes in my duffel."

"Mi casa, su casa."

Kasper went to go retrieve his bag. Not bothering to wait for him, Paxton went upstairs to take a shower. He had a lot of groveling to do. His gut had told him bringing those girls home was a bad idea, and he knew better than to ignore his gut. He had no idea how to fix this mess.

———

CORI

Damn.

She certainly hadn't expected that. Tears stung her eyes. She had to get the hell out of there. What an asshole. It hadn't even been twelve hours since they had been together. But she'd known what she was getting into. He warned her and still she gave herself to him. She also knew that she wasn't going through this again. He obviously didn't have any feelings for her.

Max pushed away from the side of his truck as she approached him. "Are they getting their asses out here?"

She took a fortifying breath. "I don't think we should count on them tonight."

He shook his head. "What did they do now?"

The screen door to Paxton's house slammed open. The two women were scurrying to their car. They peeled out of his driveway and headed toward town.

"Oh shit," Max mumbled.

She looked back at Max. "Pretty much."

"I'm sorry, Cori."

She shrugged her shoulders as she watched the women drive out of sight. She looked back at Max. "Please don't apologize for him."

With Mia still on her hip, Sloane emerged from the house. Krysta was right on her heels. She was shaking her head in disgust the whole time.

"Those rat bastards."

Sloane gave her a look. "Krysta."

"Sorry. I'll try to watch my mouth. Sorry, Mia." Krysta kissed the little girl's outstretched hand. The sound of her laughter was the sweetest thing Cori had ever heard.

Sloane handed Mia over to Max. She put her hands on her hips. "Well, ladies, it looks like it's up to us."

Max stopped making faces at his daughter and looked at Sloane. "Hey, I'm here."

She giggled. "I know you are, sweetheart." She leaned over and kissed his cheek. "You rock. Your buddies, however, are in the doghouse."

"Good, maybe you'll finally stop feeding them."

The women snickered as they entered the house together. Detective Hyland had taken the animal carcass and linens with him after they documented the scene the night before. The naked mattress taunted her. She felt uneasy just being in the room.

Sloane touched her arm. "Are you okay, honey?"

"I will be once we get this out of here."

Cori and Krysta both grabbed a different corner. They heaved the mattress up off the box spring. They were still struggling when Cori heard heavy footsteps ascending her stairs. Paxton and Kasper appeared in the doorway a moment later.

Paxton glanced over at her before turning his attention to Sloane and then Krysta. "I'm sorry."

Kasper shoved his hands in his front pockets. "Me too."

Krysta stared daggers at both men. Sloane smiled sadly as she walked over to them. She put one arm around each man's neck and hugged them. She took a step back, looking them both over.

"I love you both. Now that that's done with, please dispose of this mattress."

Without another word, Paxton and Kasper picked the mattress up like it weighed nothing and disappeared down the steps.

Sloane put her hand on Cori's shoulder. "They're both good guys. They have demons. We all do."

"I understand that, better than most. I see it every day with clients. Or at least I did before I closed my practice."

Krysta scoffed. "Don't make excuses for them. They do what they want, because they want to."

"Krysta, you know Paxton is a good man."

"I'm not saying they aren't. I'm saying they make shitty choices that hurt the people around them because they're selfish. They choose to hold onto their so-called demons. They need to learn to let shit go." Krysta pinned Sloane with a menacing look. "If you start singing that song again, I will kick your ass."

Cori didn't need to have any children to know that song. At one time it was playing everywhere. She laughed with Sloane as Krysta punched her new friend in the arm playfully.

Sloane fixed Cori with a compassionate expression. "He'll pull his head out of his ass eventually."

"I don't need him to. There's nothing between us."

"No?"

"No," Cori replied as sternly as she could muster considering it was killing her inside. Paxton's words echoed in her head: "This won't end well." She took a moment to shake the image of Paxton from her mind. Both the image of him above her and the image of him on his couch with someone else.

"I said the same thing about Max."

Krysta threw an arm around each woman's shoulders. "I say we get the new mattress up here. And by we, I mean them. Then we should grab some food and relax."

"Sounds great, but I need to get my little angel home and in bed." Sloane smiled brightly. "I know—tomorrow everyone can head over to our house. We'll have a cook-out. Cori, bring your suit to go swimming."

"Um—"

"Excellent. I'll text you the address. Come on over about lunch time." Sloane beamed.

Krysta patted Cori's arm. "Don't fight it." She laughed.

"Okay. I'll be there."

"Excellent!" Sloane yelled over her shoulder as she made her way out onto the front porch.

Cori and Krysta moved out of the doorway just in time for Paxton and Kasper to come barging through with her new mattress. They took it straight up the stairs without hesitation. Krysta looked at her and rolled her eyes. Then they joined Sloane where she stood in the yard with Mia back on her hip and an arm around Max.

They looked perfect together. Max pushed Sloane's bangs out of her face. Cori watched in awe. They looked so much in love. The way Sloane gazed up lovingly at Max, Cori finally had to look away. Her gaze found Paxton as he exited her house with Kasper trailing behind him. He never looked at her. He marched over to Max.

He took the baby from Sloane. The little girl's squeal lit his face up. His smile was warm and inviting. At that moment, Cori saw the man Paxton could have—no, *should have* been. She could see the man that wasn't damaged by his past. It was breathtaking. Her heart ached for him as she stood there mesmerized. She had to keep herself from going to him.

"He's just a man, Cori," Krysta whispered in her ear.

Cori met Krysta's stare. "What does that mean?"

"You're looking at him like he's just descended from the heavens."

"Don't be ridiculous. I'm not even sure what that means," she scoffed.

Krysta snorted. "I like you, Cori. I think if he got out of his own way, you'd be good for him. I just don't want you to get hurt."

Cori wrapped her arms around Paxton's little sister. "I appreciate that." She pulled back to look Krysta in the eye. "I plan on staying as far away from him as I can."

"You live next door," Krysta pointed out.

"So far is more of a state of mind." She chuckled. "So what's up with you and Kasper?"

She shrugged Cori off. "He's been Paxton's best friend since they were kids. We've always bickered. He thinks he's God's gift to women and I think he's an ass fuck."

Cori let it drop. Her line of work taught her how to read people better than most. She knew there was something under the surface, but what, Cori had no idea. She risked a look back to where Paxton had stood a moment ago. He was gone. She sighed deeply. No matter what she told Krysta, she knew keeping Paxton out of her head would be impossible.

"Do you want me to stay with you tonight?" Krysta gave her a sad smile.

Cori shook her head feverishly. "Absolutely not. No way. I'll be fine."

"Are you sure? I really don't mind."

"Thanks, Krysta, but you've had to babysit me enough today."

"If you change your mind, you know where to find me."

Cori hugged her goodbye. Shoving her hands into her pockets, she walked to Max and Sloane. They were still talking to Kasper.

"Thank you, guys. I really appreciate your help."

Sloane hugged her. "Anytime. If you need anything, don't hesitate to call. I left my number on your nightstand."

To her surprise, Max hugged her as well. "It was nice to meet you, Doc. Seriously, we're here if you need anything."

Max took Mia and loaded her in the car seat in the back of the truck. Once the little family was secured inside, Sloane waved from the passenger seat as Max backed out of her driveway. That left her alone on the front lawn with Kasper.

"Hey, Doc. I wanted to apologize for earlier." He actually looked ashamed for a moment. His hands were shoved into his front pockets and he was having a hard time making eye contact. It was completely at odds with the Kasper she had dealt with up until this point.

"Look, Kasper, it's none of my business what you two do. I'm his neighbor. He's helping me out, that's it."

She shrugged her shoulders like it was no big deal. Like seeing Paxton with that woman didn't crush something inside of her. She'd known before anything happened between them that it wouldn't be some Cinderella story. She didn't believe in fairy tales anyway. She'd dealt with too much real-life shit to wear rose-colored glasses.

Damn, how she wanted to, though. She *wanted* to believe a man like Paxton would sweep her off her feet. But she couldn't. It would only bring more disappointment in the future. Kasper didn't look fooled, but he kept his mouth shut. With a simple nod, Kasper walked off toward Paxton's house.

Cori high-tailed back inside her own home. She meticulously checked each room to make sure every window and door was locked up tight. She even went as far as propping a kitchen chair under all the doorknobs. *It worked in the movies*. Feeling satisfied with her high-tech security, she went upstairs to make her new bed. Before climbing into bed, she couldn't resist the urge any longer. Cori turned off the bedroom lights and walked to the window. Paxton's silhouette was encased in his window frame.

Was he looking for her? Was he checking around the house? She looked around the yard. Unfortunately, she saw shadows everywhere and it creeped her out. Were they normal shadows or was something sinister waiting for her inside of them? She dropped the curtain back into place and took a step backward. She wrapped her arms around herself, hugging tightly. She needed to chill out or she'd never get to sleep tonight. She pulled the covers back and crept into bed.

She felt like a little kid. If she pulled the covers up over her head, would she feel safer? Would she magically be invisible to monsters entering her room? Knowing she was being irrational, she pulled the covers up to her chin and snuggled into her pillow. She watched each corner of the room until her eyelids began to get heavy and closed on their own.

———

TANK

Tank stood in the window checking the perimeter of Cori's house. He had his Glock 22 tucked in his waistband, the cold metal pressing against his spine. It was comforting having it close to him, since it was the same type of gun he'd carried when he was on the police force.

He still felt like cow shit for his actions tonight. He came home waiting for her to come over and confront him for the things he did, but she didn't. She seemed indifferent. She barely looked his way. He didn't want that to bother him. *Fuck.* It did.

His phone vibrated in his back pocket. Retrieving it, he looked down at the screen. Mother.

Swiping his thumb across the screen, he accepted the call. "What's up, dude?"

"Okay, so listen to this. Since the trail on the widower went cold, I cross-checked names from Cori's practice, social media, and family with anyone using credit cards within a thirty-mile radius. Another name popped."

"How the hell did you get those names?"

"Do I ask you questions I don't really want the answer to? No, I don't. Anyway, Stanley Pickett is a longtime patient of hers. He was quite upset that she closed her practice, per the emails he's been sending her. Just so happens he checked into a motel off highway ten yesterday. That puts him, maybe, fifteen miles away from you and the good Doc."

"Okay, but why now? Where the hell has he been the past couple of days?"

"I don't know. Maybe he finally ran out of cash. Maybe he was sleeping in his car and decided he couldn't go another night without a hot shower and a bed. Who knows, man. The important thing is, we know where the bastard is now."

"True. Can you send me a picture of the guy and a

description of his car? I'll go check it out in the morning. I don't want to leave now. I don't feel comfortable leaving her alone at night."

"Is she staying with you?" The surprise in Mother's voice grated him. The fact that it grated him, grated him even more. He refused to get caught up in some girl. His gut told him that that was exactly what was beginning to happen. *Ugh.*

"No, dick weed. She's at home."

The cackle that erupted from the other end of the phone was a half laugh, half snort. Paxton couldn't not laugh along with his friend.

"You're surlier than usual. You sure there isn't something going on with this girl?"

"Just keep me updated on any movements, okay?" Paxton barked.

"You got it. I'll talk to you later."

Paxton released the breath he had been holding. "Thanks, man. Later."

Gutter Mouth looked up from his phone. "What's going on?"

"Mother found a lead. We'll go check it out in the morning."

His friend raised an eyebrow. "Not tonight?"

Paxton gritted his teeth, ready to get the third degree from another one of his buddies. "No. Not tonight."

"Okay. I'm gonna hit the sack then. See ya in the AM."

Gutter Mouth hopped up from the couch and bound up the stairs like a kid. Paxton turned back to the window, scanning the property one last time before deciding to get some shut eye himself. There was nothing he could do at this point.

He went upstairs, stopping briefly outside of Krysta's door. She never spoke to him when she came home. She went straight to her room. Should he knock and apologize? But apologize for what? Bringing a girl to his own house? He was a single man. She was his sister. She had no right to be pissed at him.

"Fuck it," he mumbled as he turned away from her door. He went to his room down the hall. Stripping down to nothing, he flopped onto his bed. The cool sheets felt like heaven against his heated skin.

He stared up at the ceiling for a while. He couldn't stop himself from wondering what Gillian wanted. Why would she come track him down now? It couldn't be to reconcile. He had been extremely blunt when he'd packed his bags to leave. He had a certified letter sent informing her of the rent he wanted or she could vacate the property. That lasted six months before she decided to move out. The very next day, Paxton put the house up for sale.

That life was over and gone. He even sold his Camaro. He didn't want anything to remind him of her, but not because he hated her for hurting him. He got rid of everything that reminded him of the good times they'd had together. Some of the best times of his life had been spent with her. Unfortunately, the idea of marrying a cop and the reality were two different things. She'd spent too many evenings eating dinner alone because he was stuck on a stakeout or had caught another case an hour before shift change.

It was the pretending to be happy to his face for months on end that pissed him off the most. He wouldn't have changed a thing about his job. He'd saved lives and reunited families. That was more important than making dinner on time. He scoffed.

It didn't matter what that bitch wanted. He rolled over onto his side. He was proud of himself when he finally pushed her memory out of his mind. However, a raven-haired beauty quickly took her place. He needed to apologize to Cori for slamming the door in her face.

TEN
TANK

PAXTON OPENED HIS EYES, surprised to find the sun up. He didn't remember falling asleep. He pushed himself up to a sitting position, stretching his arms both above his head and behind his back. He hadn't had a decent workout in a few days. He was itching to stretch his muscles out.

He pulled on a pair of basketball shorts, retrieved a pair of socks from his dresser drawer, and headed downstairs.

Krysta was at the kitchen island tapping away at her laptop. Her earbuds were in her ears—a sure sign that she wasn't yet speaking to him. He smiled big and bright when she looked up at him. She rolled her eyes before they lowered back to the computer screen. Before he left the kitchen, though, he noticed her smile slightly. She wouldn't stay mad long. She never did.

He laced up his sneakers and grabbed his iPhone off the table. Outside, Paxton put the small buds in his ears. Rock music played loudly, effectively shutting the rest of the world out. He took a song to stretch his limbs out.

Then he started a slow jog. He had a routine he used. He mapped out his paths months ago. This particular path would bring him back home after a two-mile run.

He lost himself in the music and movement of his body. He didn't need to think of where he was going. His body knew. By the time he came to a stop in his driveway, Paxton felt revitalized, his mind and body both recharged. He needed a nice cold shower to cool himself down. Then he would head out to the last place Mr. Stanley Pickett had used his credit card.

Hopefully after today, Paxton would convince the man to go back to wherever he came from. Then Paxton could go on with his life without having to worry about Cori. *Speaking of.* As if thinking of her had somehow summoned her, Cori stepped onto her porch. Her tan legs looked fantastic in a pair of spandex shorts. God help him. The white tank top ended just below her breasts, leaving her taut belly on display for his viewing pleasure.

Nonchalantly, he strolled up to his porch steps. He watched Cori out of the corner of his eye as she entered her car. Not once did she look over at him.

Krysta's voice boomed from the front door five feet away. "Damn, my big brother must be losing his touch with the ladies."

"Damn it, Krysta. You're lucky I didn't have my piece on me," he growled.

She was hunched over holding her belly, laughing. "I scared you. Admit it. And you would never shoot me, asshole."

Paxton grabbed the door handle. "Get outta the way, brat," he grumbled playfully.

Krysta moved aside while she continued to laugh and just like that, they were cool again.

Gutter Mouth came in from the kitchen with a bottle of water in one hand and a half-eaten sandwich in the other. He nodded in their direction. "What's so funny?"

Krysta stopped laughing, put her hands on her hips, and gave him a once-over. "Your face," she deadpanned.

Paxton roared with amusement at the look on Gutter Mouth's face. Krysta had always been quick-witted. So had Gutter Mouth. It was hilarious to watch the two of them go at it.

Gutter Mouth closed his mouth and narrowed his eyes at her. "Very funny, kitten."

"I have my moments." She smiled, a look of pride on her pretty face.

Gutter Mouth turned to Paxton. "Dude, are we heading over to the motel or what?"

Confusion marred Krysta's expression. "Motel?" She observed both men.

Paxton wrapped his arm around Krysta's shoulder. "Just following up on a lead."

She grinned. "I wanna go."

He shook his head at his sister. "Nope. No way. You are *not* getting involved."

"Why not? You are." She pouted.

Gutter Mouth scoffed. "It's our job."

"Oh, I forgot that Cori hired you to snoop into her life." Krysta gasped. She looked between the two men with an expression of exaggerated shock. "Wait. She *did* hire you, right?"

He stood there quietly next to Gutter Mouth. He focused his gaze on anything except his too observant little sister. Neither of them said anything to confirm or deny what she was implying. She folded her arms over her chest, no doubt waiting for one of them to answer.

"I didn't think so."

Gutter Mouth smiled. "Think of it as pro bono."

Krysta rolled her eyes. "You're so full of shit."

A lightbulb turned on in Paxton's head. "Look, you wanna help?"

"You know I do."

"Stay here and watch her. Make sure no one is trespassing on her property. If you see anyone, call me and Foster."

"Yes, sir," she replied.

"Now that's more like it." He winked playfully at her.

"Find out who's doing this, big brother. I like her."

"You know I will."

She looked at Gutter Mouth. "Hey, boy wonder." Krysta waited for Gutter Mouth to look up at her. "Watch his six for me."

"Never a doubt," he answered seriously.

Paxton grabbed his keys off the table and headed out to his truck, Gutter Mouth on his heels. They both climbed in and Paxton threw the machine into reverse. They weren't even out of Paxton's neighborhood before Gutter Mouth looked over at him seriously. Finally, Paxton couldn't take it anymore.

"What, dude? You're like a chick over there staring at me."

"She's gotten into your head. First Max. Now you."

"She has not," Paxton scoffed.

Gutter Mouth raised an eyebrow. "Oh no?"

Paxton returned his full attention to the road in front of him. Fuck yes, she'd gotten into his head. Like an insect, she'd burrowed inside like it was nothing. He didn't know what to do to get her out. She was smart and sexy and he craved to own every inch of her sweet fucking body again and again until neither of them could think straight. He wanted to be the only man she wanted. How could he though? He'd already hurt her. More than once too.

Finally, he mumbled, "Maybe."

They finished the rest of the drive in silence. Paxton pulled into an open space in front of the motel's office. It was a dingy hole in the wall. There was more than one working girl watching for potential johns while standing out in front of their rented rooms. The one closest to them ran her hand up her body, squeezing her own breast. Paxton shook his head before turning to enter the office building.

The guy working the counter looked normal enough. Short dark hair, clean shaven, and a beer gut that looked well paid for. His name tag said Porter. Maybe they would get lucky after all. Gutter Mouth put both elbows on the counter.

"Hey, man. You the manager?"

The guy looked up from what Paxton could now see was some sort of adult magazine. "Who's asking?"

Gutter Mouth stood up to his full height. "Obviously, we are. We're here on business. We're not here to jam you up over anything."

Paxton pulled a printout of Stanley Pickett's driver's license from his back pocket. He unfolded it and slammed the paper on the counter with enough force to make the manager jump. "What room is this man in?"

"I've never seen him before," the man stammered without looking at the photograph.

Paxton tried to keep his cool. He gritted his teeth. "Look again."

This time the man studied the picture. His face eased up. "I'm telling you, that dude has never come in here."

Gutter Mouth put a hand on Paxton's shoulder, silencing him. "His credit card was used here two nights ago."

"I only had two guys check in that night. He—" The clerk pointed at the photo still lying on the counter. "—was not one of them."

Gutter Mouth sounded a lot calmer than Paxton felt. "Give us the room numbers."

"No way, man. Fuck you."

Paxton took a deep breath. "I'm not fucking asking. Give us the room numbers. Right. Fucking. Now," he demanded through gritted teeth.

Gutter Mouth held up a hand and smiled mischievously. "Dude, I know what we're asking could get you in hot water. I can understand your reluctance." He took his wallet out and set a hundred-dollar bill on the counter. "So, how about I leave my friend Benjamin here for you. You can introduce him to some of those pretty ladies outside and while you do that, I can watch your sign-in book for you."

The little weasel's eyes sparkled. He licked his lips and glanced out the window. He slowly reached for the money. Once he had his prize, he pushed the book toward Gutter Mouth and quickly ran outside.

Gutter Mouth grinned like an idiot. "You catch more flies with honey, big man. Rooms 204 and 110."

Paxton barreled out of the building. He didn't wait for Gutter Mouth; he knew his friend would be right behind him. They found Room 110 first. Paxton banged on the door with the side of his fist. A man in his forties answered the door in nothing except a pair of boxer shorts, his hard-on visible through the fabric.

The man smiled invitingly at them. "You guys are late, but we'll forgive you this time."

He pushed the door open further. Paxton had a clear view of a naked man sitting on the bed with his head thrown back as another man knelt before him.

Paxton backed away from the door. "Sorry, wrong room."

"Don't be nervous. Come on in," the man called from the doorway. "We were all first timers once." Paxton and Gutter Mouth didn't look back as they headed for Room 204.

Paxton glanced at Gutter Mouth. "Do *not* tell Krysta about that. She will never let us forget about it." Paxton didn't care what those guys were doing—he just didn't want to be a part of it. Krysta would tease them both from now until eternity if she knew.

"You don't need to tell me that," he replied quickly.

They approached the second room. Gutter Mouth advanced first. "Dude, do you smell that?"

Paxton knew that smell. It smelled of death. This was not going as Paxton had planned.

"Tank, don't do anything. I'll go get keys. Wait for me. Got it?"

"Yeah," he replied absentmindedly.

What the *fuck* was going on? Even if Stanley Pickett died in his sleep last night, there wouldn't be a smell like this already.

He wanted to bust the door down. He hated waiting, and he wanted this shit wrapped up. With a fucking bow. A few moments later, Gutter Mouth jogged up to him, the motel manager walking briskly behind him.

"Open it," Paxton barked.

This time the man made no objections. He quickly

unlocked the motel room door. Both Paxton and Gutter Mouth pulled their guns from their holsters. The clerk actually squealed before cowering behind the nearest car.

The smell was stronger without the door as a barrier. Paxton had been to enough crime scenes to know this person hadn't died during the night. They moved inside slowly. Paxton checked behind the door and under the beds as Gutter Mouth immediately moved toward the back of the room to check the bathroom and closet.

Once they cleared the room, Gutter Mouth called the station, asking for Foster directly. Paxton stood above the decaying body of Stanley Pickett, which had a blue hue and was slightly bloated. Foam surrounded the deceased's mouth. *Fuck.* It wasn't impossible that Pickett had been stalking Cori, but judging by the bloodied remains of his skull, someone had taken care of the problem for them days ago. But why? Who? And if that was the case…who had been peeking into Cori's window yesterday?

Now they were back at square one in finding out who was responsible. Paxton scrubbed his face with his hands. He was anxious to get home to check on Cori. Now he was grateful that he left instructions for Krysta to watch out for her. He had only suggested it to keep Krysta from pouting and trying to tag along, but at least he knew she would be safe since they couldn't leave the scene before Foster and the other boys in blue arrived.

The first car to pull in was occupied by Foster and his partner, Brody. Brody was a real asshat and Sloane's ex-boyfriend. It made times like these slightly awkward. He didn't know how Foster worked with him every day since Foster was married to Sloane's cousin, Bella. Gutter Mouth, on the other hand, had no problem getting some form of entertainment from the whole situation.

Gutter Mouth strolled over to Foster, shaking his hand. "Hey, man. How's it going?"

Foster grinned like a fool. "Good. Bella is pregnant again."

Paxton shook Foster's hand. "Wow. That was fast. How old is Seth now?"

"He just turned six months old."

Gutter Mouth fist bumped him. "You old dog, you."

They both laughed at Foster's smug expression. Brody walked over to them after checking with the other cops inside of the motel room.

"Hey guys." He focused his attention on Foster. "I sent some guys door-to-door for a canvass. In this neighborhood, though, I doubt we get anything."

They all nodded in agreement. No one would talk to the police here. They'd have to wait and see if the forensics tech and the coroner found anything. That could take days or even weeks to get any answers.

"So, Brody." Gutter Mouth smiled. "How are things going with you?"

Brody crossed his arms and eyed Gutter Mouth suspiciously. "Going okay. You?"

"Great. Abso-fuckin-lutley fantastic. I was hanging out with Mia yesterday..." He grinned mischievously. "...you know who Mia is, don't you?"

"Who?"

"Gutter Mouth," Paxton warned.

Gutter Mouth always liked to stir the shit pot. One day —when Paxton wasn't there to reel him in—someone was going to make him lick the spoon.

"Mia. Sloane and Max's daughter."

Brody looked like a little kid that'd been told "no." His

head hung slightly before he nodded his head in Foster's direction.

"Yeah, Foster mentioned she had a baby a while ago."

Brody walked away without another word. Foster smacked Gutter Mouth in the back of the head. "Dude. You and your big ass mouth."

Gutter Mouth looked appalled. It was comical to see that particular expression on his best friend's face. "What did *I* do?"

Paxton pointed his finger at him. "You. You opened your big fat mouth. He doesn't need to know shit."

"I was just…shit, you're right."

Paxton sighed. "Can we please hurry this up. I'd like to get back to Cori and let her know what's going on."

Foster clapped his shoulder. "Go on, man. I've got everything I need from you. I know where to find you if I have any other questions."

"Thanks, brother. Gutter Mouth, let's roll."

On the drive back, Paxton kept going over all of the information he had. At this point he wasn't certain of much. The perp was a white male; he knew that from the limited description Cori was able to give after he was seen peeping in her window. He knew it hadn't been Stanley Pickett, but he had shit else to go on. He would have to wait a while to hear from friends he still had at the lab on whether there'd been fingerprints or DNA left behind.

Gutter Mouth was the first one to break the silence. "What do you think?"

Paxton rubbed the back of his neck. "We're missing something. Or we overlooked something."

"We don't have enough to go on in order to miss something. Did you ask the Doc?"

"She said she didn't know."

"Did you believe her?" Gutter Mouth asked with a hint of disbelief in his voice.

"Not really."

Gutter Mouth raised an eyebrow. "Not really?"

"No. I didn't believe her," Paxton growled.

"Then what the hell? Why aren't we questioning her?"

"Questioning her? Like a criminal?"

His best friend held up his hand defensively. "Dude, I know you're sweet on this girl and I totally approve. She's hot and smart, I'd go for it. What I'm saying is, we have a job to do and we can't do it without all of the information pertaining to it."

"Krysta is right though; we weren't hired for a job. Cori never actually asked for my help."

Neither of them said anything else. After what happened yesterday, how could Paxton grill her for not telling him whatever she knew? In her eyes, he was no doubt a womanizing prick.

Which wasn't entirely true. Wasn't entirely false either. *Fuck.* Of course, this was her safety they were talking about. He knew he would do anything to keep her safe.

They pulled up to the house just as Krysta was backing out of the driveway. He could make out Cori in the passenger seat. Did something happen? After throwing the truck in park, he jumped out, charging for Krysta's car.

"What happened?"

Krysta stopped before pulling out onto the street. She looked at him like he was crazy. "Nothing. Why?"

"Then why the hell are you leaving like something was chasing you? Where are you going?"

"To Sloane and Max's. They're having a cookout."

Paxton wasn't told of any cookout. He wondered if it

had to do with his behavior the night before. *Duh, asshole.* Of course it did.

"Do you really think that's a good idea?"

"Gee...let's think. Should I take her someplace secluded and safe, where there will be a bunch of ex-cops to watch over her, or sit in the house that she's being terrorized in all by ourselves?"

"Fine. I'll see you there soon," he growled.

"Okay."

Krysta started backing up again.

"Krysta," he yelled.

She finished straightening her car out. "Yeah?"

He scowled. "Slow the fuck down."

She gave him a shit-eating grin before peeling out. He was going to kill her later. Gutter Mouth stood next to him and patted his shoulder.

"Your sister is a pain in the ass, dude."

"Tell me something I don't know."

CORI

The Fear property was beautiful. The farm-style house stood proudly at the end of a gravel driveway, with a white, wraparound porch standing out against the brick-colored wood. Cori took in the surrounding area. Trees grew all along the back and sides, creating a peaceful and secluded sanctuary. Krysta drove around to the back of the house. There was a large parking area that was fairly full.

Krysta looked over at her, a big smile on her face. "Grab your stuff—they're probably already down by the pond."

"Pond?"

"You're gonna love it," she called over the hood of the car. "Max did it after Sloane moved in with him. It's amazing."

Cori snatched her bag from the back seat and caught up with Krysta. They followed a worn dirt path away from the house. She could hear laughter coming from the trees ahead. They had only gone a few feet into the woods when a clearing opened in front of them. Cori could see Max in the water holding Mia on his shoulders. The little girl was in a white, one-piece bathing suit with a large white hat on. The huge brim flopped down slightly. Sloane was standing in front of them, laughing.

Cori looked around in awe. It was like an oasis in the middle of the woods. There were hanging lights all around, strung on trees, poles, and umbrellas. It looked like there were small spotlights sitting near the water's edge too—she assumed for night swimming. The pond was fairly large in diameter. Cori couldn't believe the work that must've went into creating this place.

"Hi guys," Sloane hollered from the water.

Krysta waved. "Hey, hon."

Sloane left the water and scurried over to them. She hugged them both. Cori grew up without many female friends. Certainly none of them had been close enough of a friend to hug her. It was a little weird, but at the same time comforting.

Sloane took her hand and began leading her to one of the three picnic tables that were spread around the clearing. There were a few people seated there. Cori felt anxious. She wasn't shy, but she was more of a one-on-one kind of person.

"Guys, this is Cori. She's Tank's neighbor. Cori, this is Mother."

"Mother?" Cori asked.

Mother sat there with a knowing smile on his face. His gray eyes sparkled behind the black-framed glasses he wore. His hair was dark and cut short. He reached across the table to shake her hand.

The smile never left his face. "Nickname. Most of us have one. Nice to meet you, Doc."

She returned the smile and the handshake. "It's nice to meet you too."

"And this," Sloane continued, "is my cousin, Bella. She's married to Foster. He should be here soon. The little one in the playpen is Seth."

"Foster? Detective Hyland?"

Bella smiled at her. "That's him. It's nice to put a face to the name. How are you doing?"

"I could be better," Cori answered honestly.

Bella's smile faltered slightly. "Well, you can relax while you're here. This is one place where you're completely safe."

"Thank you."

Sloane motioned to the two other women at the table. "This is Joy and Iris. They're friends of Mother's."

They both nodded toward Cori, but they never said a word. They looked like they could be sisters. Both had platinum blonde hair and green eyes. They ignored everyone else and went back to fawning on Mother. Cori smiled and rolled her eyes at Sloane.

Krysta put her arm around Cori. "Let's go get changed." She pointed to the other side of the clearing. "There's a changing room over there."

There was a small building slightly bigger than the shed Cori had in her yard. Krysta went inside first. Cori watched everyone while she waited. Sloane was putting Mia into the playpen with Seth. Mother had joined Max in the water. They leaned against the bank, each with a beer in their hand. The future Stepford wives sat close by giggling.

Krysta exited the changing room after just a few moments. She was gorgeous in a baby blue bikini. The color brought her eyes to life while contrasting against the dark chestnut hue of her hair. She had a body of an athlete. Although muscular, she was still feminine.

"Wow, Krysta. You look amazing."

Krysta beamed. "Thanks. Go on and get changed. A dip in the pond will help relax you."

Cori let herself inside of the one-room building. She was surprised by the décor she found. It was gorgeous. The room was the color of sand. There was a blue chaise lounge that ran the length of one wall. Beautiful emerald green pillows in multiple sizes adorned it. She set her bag down. Cori ran her hand over the smooth fabric before sitting down to remove her shoes. On the other side of the room there was a sort of shelving unit.

Within it, multiple large canvas boxes were stored. They were in multiple colors. Curious, she peeked inside of one. There were a pair of shoes and what looked like a change of clothes inside. The one next to it contained the bag that Krysta had brought with her. Now that the mystery of the multicolored bins was solved, Cori finished removing her clothes and retrieved her suit from her bag.

She wore a bright red one-piece. The suit was designed with the sides cut away, giving it an hourglass appearance. She looked at herself in the full-length mirror that hung on the back of the door. Everything was where it was supposed to be, and she thought she looked pretty good. She tucked her bag into one of the empty bins and joined Krysta.

Krysta's eyes widened as she looked her over. "Holy hell. My brother is gonna shit when he sees you."

Krysta had a maniacal laugh that you couldn't resist joining in on when you heard it. They sat on the edge of the pond, their feet dangling into the cool, clear water. Cori removed a hair tie from her wrist and pulled her hair up into a loose bun. The breeze felt like heaven on her overheated neck.

Krysta eyed her suspiciously. "How do you do that?"

"Do what?" Cori answered, slightly confused.

"How do you do that messy bun look? When I try, it always looks like a bird attacked my head before building its nest in my hair."

They both laughed as they sat there together. Being with Krysta reminded her of times she spent growing up with her own sister. She missed her. Once this whole mess was behind her, she should have her for a visit. Even better, maybe she should leave town and visit her instead. Closing her eyes, she lay back on the soft grass. She could feel the sun soaking into her skin and the water continuously lapping around her calves. It had a wonderful calming effect on her.

She wasn't sure how long she lay there before the warm kiss of the sun's rays disappeared from her face. She didn't bother opening her eyes to see the person eclipsing her sun.

"If you don't mind. You're blocking the sun."

"No, I don't mind."

The deep, throaty voice that responded sent shivers up her spine. It was something only Paxton could do to her.

Opening her eyes, she looked up at the beast towering above her. The way the sun hit his back illuminated the outline of his body while disguising his features. He looked mysterious and dangerous.

Cori pushed up onto her elbow and used her other hand to shield her eyes from the sun. At this angle, she could make out the rough stubble that adorned Paxton's face. He had on a baseball hat with Fear Incorporated's logo on it. Damn, she loved a man in a hat. Once again the man had no shirt on. Since they were at a pond for swimming, she couldn't mentally sigh at his lack of clothing. But it did remind her of another time she had to look up at him with no shirt on.

She felt her cheeks heat up as she pushed herself up off the ground. She still had to look up to him, but not in such a familiar way as when she was propped up on her elbow. He gave her a little smirk. Obviously, he remembered too. She was about to tell him to wipe it off his face when Kasper bounded over to them.

"Hey, Doc. Lookin' good." He waggled his eyebrows.

Cori knew she was blushing. She could feel the heat blossom on her cheeks again. She shook her head, hoping to brush him off. His gaze swung over to Krysta.

He winked at her. "Hey, kitten."

In a soft, sweet voice, Krysta replied, "Lick my ass, Kasper."

"Krysta," Paxton scolded. "What the hell. Don't say shit like that."

She laughed. "Like what?"

"You know what. Aren't you supposed to be a lady?"

"Please," she scoffed. "Growing up around you two? That would've been a miracle."

Kasper smiled. "She has a point."

"Both of you shut up."

Krysta glanced over at Cori. A mischievous smile painted her lips. "While you guys decide what a lady should or shouldn't say, Cori and I are going to get wet."

Paxton groaned while Cori laughed loudly. Kasper shook his head in amusement. Krysta looped her arm through Cori's and together they entered the water. They stopped advancing toward the center of the pond as the water reached their waists.

Krysta nodded toward the guys. "Look at them."

"What?"

"So smug all the time. Sometimes it's fun to rattle their cages."

Cori watched the two blonde woman sashay over to them. Kasper immediately wrapped an arm around the one girl's waist. The other girl linked her arms through Paxton's. She pressed up against him.

"They don't look rattled. They look busy."

Krysta scooped water up in her hands. "Don't let that scene fool you. You want my big brother's undivided attention?"

Cori opened her mouth to answer. Before she could utter a word, Krysta flung her water-filled hands at her. Cold water splashed Cori's front. She squealed in surprise. Krysta was laughing so hard, she actually snorted. That prompted Cori to join in. They continued to splash each other. Cori was having such a great time, she forgot the guys were even there.

A masculine voice bellowed, "Cannonball!" just moments before the water seemed to explode next to Cori. Max's body erupted from the water. He shook his head wildly like a dog. Droplets flew from his hair, spraying the girls.

He laughed with them. "You guys having a good time?"

Cori nodded. "Yes, thank you for having me."

"Anytime, Doc." Max winked lightheartedly before swimming back to the water's edge. Sloane handed him baby Mia before she entered the pond. Cori admired the little family. Someday she hoped to have one of her own.

Across the clearing a man walked in their direction. He was carrying a stack of something, but he was too far away for Cori to make out who he was.

The man yelled, "Food's here."

As he made his way to the picnic table closest to the pond, she finally recognized the man. Detective Hyland. He set down what looked like a dozen pizza boxes and kissed his wife. Everyone congregated around the table, waiting their turn at the boxes filled with gooey cheesiness. Cori was a pizza junky. She couldn't wait to eat.

Krysta put an arm around her shoulder. "Let's grab some grub before those animals eat it all."

"I'm in."

———

TANK

Cori was as distracting as ever. The blonde hanging on his arm couldn't hold a candle to her. What the hell was she thinking when she put on that bathing suit? It wasn't skimpy or overly revealing like his damn sister's was, but holy hell it was sexy on her. He stood on the side of the picnic table that was facing the pond. He had a perfect view of her as she exited the water with Krysta. Droplets of water on her skin sparkled like diamonds in the sunlight as they slid down her exposed skin. He wanted to lick them away.

Her dark hair was piled up on her head, exposing the curve of her neck. He couldn't decide if he liked it better up or down. The women were smiling and laughing as they approached the picnic table covered in pizza boxes.

Gutter Mouth elbowed him in the ribs. "Dude, knock that shit off. You're embarrassing."

"What the fuck are you talking about?"

"You're practically drooling."

"Whatever." Paxton dismissed him. Returning his attention to the girls, he called out to his sister. "Can't you wear something with a little more fabric?"

"I could." She grinned. "Although that doesn't seem to matter in Cori's case."

What the hell? Did everyone know he had been checking Cori out? He glanced around at his friends. Sloane was trying to hide her smile. Max was not. *Asshole.* He didn't think Foster and Bella were paying any attention to anyone except themselves until Foster winked at him. Cori's face was pink from the blush creeping across her cheeks.

He liked that. He liked that *he* was the one who made her blush even more. She looked away quickly, avoiding eye contact with him. No matter—he would be better off if he could get her out of his mind. She was already taking up entirely too much space in there.

He pilfered a few slices of pepperoni from the nearest box and took it over to the table that Mother was sitting at.

Mother nodded his head in the girls' direction. "Your sister is looking good, man."

Paxton stopped in his tracks, the piece of pizza only an inch from his lips. His eyes raised to meet his friend's.

"Dude, don't *even* think about it," he replied through gritted teeth.

"You need to chill out, Tank. I'm not gonna chase after Krysta. I was simply viewing her as one would a painting. Strictly looking."

"Well, stop looking," he grumbled as he took a bite of his pizza. His sister was off limits. He focused on eating his pizza before he said anything else and made an ass out of himself.

Mother chuckled from his spot across from him. Paxton didn't see what was so funny. He didn't want his sister with one of his buddies. He knew how these guys were. Krysta put on a tough façade, but she was a good girl with a big heart.

Paxton glanced over at the table she was sitting at with Cori. Gutter Mouth was saying something that awarded him the middle finger from Krysta. Cori was laughing as Krysta put her arm around her shoulder. Those two had become close friends quickly.

Paxton liked that they got along so well. Krysta needed more female friends. He continued to sneak peeks in their direction. Cori's smile captivated him every time. There was just something about her that called out to him. It was nice to see her enjoying herself.

Gutter Mouth plopped down next to him. "Well, the Doc is all yours. She obviously has no taste in real men," he joked.

Paxton grinned. "I'll show you a real man."

Gutter Mouth pointed toward Cori. "It's not me you need to prove it to."

She was walking toward the changing room. Was she leaving? Paxton jumped up from his seat fast enough that he just knew he'd hear about it later. He didn't care. He needed to talk to her. He needed…hell, he didn't know what he needed. He charged after her. She opened the door to the changing room and stepped inside. Paxton grabbed ahold of the door before she could close it all the way.

She gave a small squeal as he pulled the door back open. "What the—"

"It's just me. We need to talk."

She turned away from him. "I don't think we do." She walked farther into the small room.

Since she didn't tell him to get out, he entered and closed the door behind him. He wasn't sure what to say, but he knew he had to say something.

"I'm sorry, Doc."

"What are you sorry for? For bringing home another woman hours after we were together? Or are you sorry that we walked in on you?"

"Honestly?"

She put her hands on her perfect hips. "No, lie to me." She rolled her eyes. "Of course I want you to be honest."

He shrugged his shoulders. "Both. I shouldn't have brought that girl home. I really didn't even want to, but I did. I never meant for you to know. Believe it or not, I never wanted to hurt you."

She let out a sad sigh. "I actually believe you. I knew the situation going in. Seeing it firsthand so soon was a little more than I expected, that's all. Apology accepted."

Cori wrapped her arms around herself. The air was cooler in here and he could see the gooseflesh on her skin. He went over to the wall of bins and pulled a clean fluffy towel from one. Opening it up, he walked toward Cori. He put the towel around her, bringing their bodies incredibly close.

"You can go now," she squeaked out in a barely heard whisper.

He could smell the suntan lotion on her skin. Her eyes stayed focused straight ahead. Either she found his chest fascinating or she was purposely avoiding eye contact. Still fisting the ends of the towel, he pulled her flush up against his body. Her hands went to his chest and she looked up at him wide eyed.

Fuck it.

He leaned his head down, capturing her soft lips. Paxton swallowed her gasp of surprise. He briefly wondered if he had made a mistake. Thankfully, Cori wrapped her arms around his neck and returned his kiss feverishly. His hands roamed her body freely. He slid both hands into the holes at her sides. Gliding them over the round globes of her ass, he kneaded the soft skin with his fingertips.

Her soft moans cheered him on. He reached one hand up, grasping the knot of hair on the top of her head. He used it as leverage to move her head to the side. Paxton trailed openmouthed kisses down the side of her neck. He nipped gently at her shoulder. His other hand pressed her tighter against his erection. Cori's body melted into him. She was like putty in his hands. He removed his other hand from the back of her bathing suit and began slowly sliding the straps off both of her shoulders.

Paxton let go of her hair, which was now falling from its bun. He released her from their kiss too. Her lips were red and swollen. This time she looked him right in the eye. Passion raged inside of her gaze. He continued to pull the red fabric down her body. Her nipples instantly hardened in the air-conditioned room. Paxton took one into his mouth while pulling on the other.

He switched to the other nipple, giving it the attention he knew it needed. He looked up at Cori. Her eyes stayed fixed on him. Pleasure painted her face. He grasped both breasts, squeezing them as he trailed kisses in the valley between them. He kissed down to her belly button before removing the bathing suit completely. Her fingertips hesitantly touched his cheek.

Paxton's gaze slowly met hers. She worried her bottom lip between her teeth. Her fingers curved under his chin. She exerted only a small amount of pressure, but he understood what she wanted. He rose back up to his full height. Cori placed her hands on his chest again. Her soft lips touched on the swirl of one of his tattoos. Her tongue traced the pattern, sending chills down his spine with the simplicity and tenderness in her touch.

Her hands went for the drawstring on his trunks. The anticipation was driving him insane. He needed to get a condom from the bin with all of his things, but he wouldn't stop this woman from removing his shorts for anything in the world. The material fell from his hips, pooling around his bare feet. Her hand wrapped around him, squeezing slightly.

"Mmmm." He moaned aloud as his head fell back.

Cori stopped stroking him. "Shit," she whispered.

Paxton opened his eyes. "What's wrong?"

"I don't have anything."

He smiled before retrieving his wallet from the bin that held his belongings. He removed a gold foil circle and tossed his wallet haphazardly to the floor. She plucked the condom from his hand and tore the packaging open. After gliding the latex over him, she pushed him back onto the small couch. Paxton sat there slightly surprised at her need to be in control. He enjoyed it immensely. He sat there with his back pressed against the cool wall, waiting for her to make her move.

Cori kneeled on the couch and straddled him. She took his cock in her hand and guided him inside of her. *Fuck.* She felt absolutely amazing. She worked his cock slowly, like she had all the time in the world. Like they weren't in a changing room with a dozen people just outside of the door. Her nails dug into his shoulders as she held onto him. She rose and fell in a perfect rhythm to keep him teetering right on the end. Her soft moans did nothing to help him keep his shit together.

Paxton was buried as deep as he could be inside of her and yet it still didn't seem like it was enough. He was on the edge of something. Yes, he was close to coming, but that wasn't it. She repositioned her legs so that her knees stayed where they were, but her feet rested on the inside of his thighs. Her pussy squeezed him even tighter. His eyes closed and his head thumped against the wall. Now he couldn't think at all. He could only feel.

Her hands slid from his shoulders to his neck. Her touch felt like a cool fire. Burning, yet soothing at the same time. She cupped his chin, her hands working in unison. The pads of her thumbs caressed his cheeks.

"Paxton," she whispered like a fucking prayer.

He opened his eyes. She looked like an angel—a beautiful fucking angel sent just for him. His eyes locked with hers and *boom*. It was like when he'd taken a bullet to the knee. That sudden burst of *what the fuck* before the actual pain set in. Only it wasn't pain he was feeling now. Cori pulled his head forward. She crushed her lips to his. His beautiful angel was about to lose it. It was evident in the feverish way she kissed him. He cupped the back of her head, returning her punishing kisses with his own.

His other hand went to the small of her back. He held her to him hard. He thrust up into her as she ground her hips down onto him. Working together to get where they both desperately needed to. Suddenly Cori's muffled cries came a moment before she did. He could feel each aftershock of her orgasm around his cock. He couldn't wait any longer. He had already shown herculean strength by holding it this long. Paxton let himself go. His orgasm ripped out of his body.

"Fuck," he cried out.

He wrapped his arms around her waist and buried his head in her breasts. Still he kept coming. Cori rubbed her hands across his head and back.

She whispered against the shell of his ear, "That's it, baby. Give it all to me."

He squeezed her tighter to him. He had just finished the longest fucking orgasm of his life and he couldn't chance her getting up right away. He needed to hold her. He needed what she was giving him. He leaned back, stealing a look at her face. She looked well sated. Paxton snatched the towel from the end of the couch and wrapped it around them. Cori laid her head on his shoulder as he snaked his arms around her.

The beating of her heart gave him a sense of calmness. A peacefulness he hadn't felt in as long as he could remember. As he rubbed his hands up and down her towel-covered back, he suddenly had this crazy impulse to tell her he loved her.

What the fuck! He was torn between pushing her off him and holding her tighter. He couldn't figure out what was wrong with him. Cori lifted her head off his shoulder and gazed up at him. She placed her hand gently on his cheek.

She kissed his lips tenderly. "Thank you. That was wonderful, but I've really got to be going."

"Going?" he asked as Cori got up from his lap and retrieved her clothes from her own bin.

"Yeah. Why do you think I was coming in here? I was leaving. Mother made some calls earlier and I have someone coming over to put in an alarm system. I hope I'm not too late now." She grabbed her cell phone and checked the time before tossing it into her purse.

"Why the fuck didn't anyone tell me?" Paxton could feel his blood start to boil.

She shrugged her shoulders at him before tugging her t-shirt over her head. "I don't know, Paxton. I guess I never thought to tell you."

He watched her slide her shorts up her silky legs. Damn. She was sexy as hell even when she was putting clothes on...something he missed last time because he hauled ass out of her house.

He needed to ignore the way she made him feel. He was mad at her, damn it. He was gonna have words with Mother too.

Cori stopped with her hand on the door. She looked back at him. "Goodbye, Paxton."

Then she walked out, leaving him sitting there naked. Worse than naked, the condom was still hanging on his dick. He removed it and tossed it in the trash. After cleaning himself up, he slipped his shorts back on. Plopping himself back on the couch, he sat there dazed. What the fuck had just happened? He felt...well, he almost felt *used*. Then he was hit with a realization that he didn't want to admit. Was that how Cori had felt after he left her still lying on her kitchen table? *Fuck*. This was a disaster.

He usually liked it when women left first. He could

avoid the messy aftermath of asking them to leave or making up an excuse of some place he had to go. Paxton jumped to his feet and went looking for Cori. He spotted Mother talking to Gutter Mouth. He charged over to them.

He was getting angrier with each step he took. "Dude, what the hell?"

Mother looked perplexed. "What's wrong?"

"Why didn't you tell me about the security system you're having installed in Cori's place today?"

His friend held a hand up in a stopping motion. "Hold up. I have people install security systems all the time and never run them by you."

Paxton fisted his hands by his sides, and he clenched his teeth together with such force that they actually hurt. "That's different."

Mother smirked. "How so?"

He knew what he was implying and he wasn't taking the bait. "It just is."

"I thought you, of all people, would be happy about this. She'll have the added protection she needs and you can stop babysitting. I had to pull a lot of strings to have someone come out right away."

Paxton scrubbed his hand across his face. "I am. I wanted to be there to oversee things and to have time to vet the installer."

"Fuck you too."

Paxton immediately felt bad after hearing the wounded tone in Mother's voice. "I didn't mean it that way. Look, I'm sorry."

Gutter Mouth laughed, finally joining the conversation. "She's got you all twisted up. The great Tank has finally met his equalizer."

"I don't know what the hell you're talking about,"

Paxton growled. He surveyed the clearing, expecting Cori to be talking with Krysta or Sloane. He didn't see her anywhere. "Where the hell is she, anyway?"

Mother watched the ground at his feet while Gutter Mouth focused his attention up at the clouds. *What the fuck.* Paxton scanned the clearing again. Krysta was back in the water with Sloane and Bella. Where was Cori? Realization hit him like a freight train.

"You let her leave? Alone?"

Gutter Mouth put his hand on Paxton's shoulder. "She's a grown ass woman, Tank. She said she didn't want a ride. I guess just before she changed she called a cab because there was one waiting as soon as she came out of that room."

Mother nodded in agreement. "Besides, where the hell were *you*?"

Paxton stomped away. He could hear his so-called friends laughing behind him. He stood at the edge of the water and took a deep breath. "Krysta," he hollered.

She waded over to stand in front of him. "Did you fuck up again?"

"What?"

"I saw you go in after her. Then I saw her leave. Alone."

He sneered at his sister. "You don't know anything that went on between us. *My* question is, why did you let her leave?"

Krysta's smile slipped from her lips. A look of concern washed over her face and it turned his stomach. "Leave? Like in, she left the property?"

"Yes."

She scurried out of the water. "Paxton, I swear I told her not to go anywhere alone. I thought she might have gone to the main house to put some distance between the two of you."

"Shit."

"Where could she go? Who took her?"

He sighed. "According to Mother, she called a cab and went home to have an alarm system put in."

"Let me grab my stuff, I'll go be with her."

No way was he staying here. "I'm coming with you. Gutter Mouth can bring my truck later."

"Do you think that's smart?" she asked.

He glared at her. "Do you think I care?"

"Good point."

He watched her rush to the changing room. While she changed, he tossed Gutter Mouth his keys and told him his plan. Krysta was back out before he made it to where the trail back to the main house was located. She still had on her bathing suit, only she'd added shorts to go with it. She jogged up to him with her bag over her shoulder.

"Let's go."

ELEVEN
CORI

CORI WALKED BRISKLY BACK toward the main house. Her hands gripped the straps of her bag so tightly, her fingers were cramping. She couldn't believe she'd just walked out on Paxton. It had taken every drop of willpower she'd had. Now there was barely enough left to keep the tears at bay. She rounded the side of the house, making her way to the front. The cab driver was standing in front of the passenger's side door already.

"About time," he mumbled.

Cori rolled her eyes. "Sorry."

The driver opened the door to the back seat. She climbed in and rattled off her address after he took his seat behind the wheel. She kept replaying her encounter with Paxton. She'd sworn to herself that she wouldn't have sex with him again and look what happened. The first chance she got, she climbed right into his lap. Literally. That wasn't her. She was the analytical one. Her sister was the impulsive one.

She wasn't a booty call. Not in the past and certainly

not now. But she couldn't seem to help herself with him. She was drawn to him like a moth to the flame.

She really didn't have the money to move again...she could stay with Brianna for a little while. No. That would drive her insane. Her sister was way too flighty. They would butt heads something terrible. She would just have to show a little restraint where the grumpy giant was concerned.

She was grateful for Mother setting her up with a guy to put in a security system. She would feel much safer at night knowing she had something in place to deter anyone should they attempt to enter her house again. Perhaps she should get a dog too. A guard dog of sorts to have outside with her while gardening?

She thought of Paxton again. She closed her eyes and remembered the way he held her this last time. It was different. She felt like there was a connection. Then again, she'd felt a connection the first time they'd had sex and not only did he walk away easily enough, he picked up another woman only a few hours later. She was lost in the memory of their recent encounter when the cab driver's annoying voice broke her free.

"Lady. We're here. Hey, you hear me?"

She scowled. "Yes, I hear you. You're loud enough."

Cori handed him some cash and opened her door. He peeled out of there like his ass was on fire. She shook her head and rolled her eyes again. She kept an eye on her surroundings as she walked up to the front door, her key already in hand. Once inside, she shut and locked the door. Peering out of the front window, she noticed a white box truck parked two houses down. She hadn't noticed it before. Obviously watching her surroundings was not her strong suit.

She was halfway to the kitchen when the doorbell rang. Her blood froze. Realizing how stupid she was, she back-tracked to the door. Leaving the chain on, she opened the door an inch. A guy with thick-framed glasses in his late thirties stood on the other side. He was dressed nicely and carried a clipboard. He smiled warmly at her.

"Dr. Transue?"

"Yes."

"Hi. I'm George." He motioned to his name tag. "I'm here to install a system for your home."

Relieved, she let out the breath she'd been holding. "Sure. One moment."

Cori closed the door to remove the security chain. George was still smiling as she reopened the door. "Thank you for coming so quickly on such short notice."

"No problem, Ma'am."

"Do you need anything from me?" He was staring at her, the smile never leaving his face. It was a little off-putting, if she was being honest.

Finally, he surveyed the room. "Is there anyone else in the house?"

Cori was starting to get a weird vibe from this guy. "Does that matter?"

"Not really."

"Okay. Well, I'm going to go make a phone call. Let me know if you need anything."

She seized her purse off the coffee table and began searching inside for her cell phone. She felt the plastic case brush against her fingertips at the exact moment an arm snaked across her shoulders. Cori started thrashing her body around. She was trying desperately to break free from the stranger's grasp. She glimpsed a rag out of the corner of her eye. He was trying to put it on her face. *What the hell?* She screamed out as she turned her head from side to side. She had dropped her purse so getting to her phone now was out of the question.

He struggled to gain a better grip on her. "Hold still, bitch," he sneered.

If she could get free and get outside, she felt she'd be safe. She kicked her foot backwards, trying to connect with any part of him. Nothing except air. She tried again. And again. Still she couldn't seem to hit him as she continued to wiggle. Finally, she stomped on his foot with all of her strength. He grunted and his grip slipped just slightly, but it was enough for her to wiggle free.

Cori scrambled for the front door. Her unwanted guest swung at her and in the process he lost his balance. He fell to the ground. As he did, his hand shot out, finding purchase on her ankle.

She felt her body falling forward, then she hit the floor hard. The palms of her hands and her knees stung from scratching against the wood. She kicked and flailed as he pulled her back toward him. Each time she gained an inch, he pulled her back two.

This time, he used the momentum of her kick to flip her body over. Cori was now on her back trying unsuccessfully to crab walk to safety. He scaled up her body. She clamped her eyes closed as tight as she could. She prayed this was just a dream and she would wake up soon. Tears began to stream down her face.

His face was only inches from hers, and she could feel him panting against her skin while he looked at her. *Stay calm.* She slowly opened her eyes.

He was smiling at her. The mustache on his face was peeling up at the end. Now Cori could tell he was wearing a wig with the way it had twisted on his head in their struggle. Who was this man and what had she done to him?

She swallowed her fear down. "Who are you? What do you want with me?"

"Sweetheart, I want to be with you. We belong together," he spoke to her softly, like a lover.

Caressing her face, he leaned down like he was going to kiss her. She had nowhere to go. His body weight held her down. She turned her head to the side, and he adjusted his course. She turned to the other side to avoid his mouth. The man grabbed her face between his thumb and forefingers so hard she thought her jaw might crack. He brutally pressed his lips to hers. She wanted to vomit. She could feel his teeth behind his lips from the pressure he was using. That gave her an idea.

She tried pleading with him. "Please let me go. I won't tell anyone."

"I've waited too long to have you. I'm not letting you go now, Cori."

When his kiss began to soften, Cori quickly bit his lip as hard as she could. He screamed, but didn't budge.

"You stupid woman!" he screeched in her face. He grabbed her hair and began hitting her head against the floor. "You belong to me now. This is your fault. You remember that."

Each sentence was louder than the last. Black spots blurred her vision with each thump of her head. Pain lanced through her skull. She fought to keep herself focused. Eventually everything was black.

———

LUKE

He picked Cori up from the living room floor and heaved her over his shoulder. He couldn't believe his timing when he'd arrived earlier. Fate had him on the front porch when an installation tech showed up at the house. It was surprisingly easy to get the guy to show him his equipment.

Once they were at the tech's van, Luke tasered him and tossed him in the back. Once he was unconscious, Luke took his uniform off, then slit his throat. After that, he just had to wait for sweet Cori to arrive home.

He dumped her onto her bed and stripped her down to her bra and panties. God, she was a beautiful creature. Like a wild horse needing to be tamed. He spread her eagle, tying each limp to a corner of the bed frame. Once he knew she was secure, Luke was free to clean up some of his mess. First, he moved the tech's van the next street over. Then he had to run back to get Cori's car. He drove that a few blocks away and left it in a parking lot.

This way, when muscle head came home, he'd think she'd left. He'd snuck back inside to wait for Sleeping Beauty to come to.

————

CORI

Cori woke up from the worst nightmare she'd ever had. She didn't remember going to bed. She lowered her arms from above her head, only she couldn't bring them down more than an inch or two. She soon realized she couldn't move her legs any more than her arms. Reluctantly, she opened her eyes.

She was in her bed, her arms and legs tied to the bed frame. She had been stripped down to her bra and panties. The good news was she was alone. The bad news: She didn't know for how long. That was what really scared her. It was almost dark now. Would Paxton come looking for her? The way she'd walked out on him, he probably wouldn't ever want to see her again. So she was on her own. How would she get out of this?

She tugged against her restraints. The rope cut into her wrists and ankles. She wanted to cry out, but she didn't. She didn't want her attacker to know she was awake if he didn't already.

There was something familiar about the man. She felt like she knew him—he *did* use her name. Then again, if he had been stalking her, it would make sense he would know it either way.

She lay still, hoping to conserve her energy for any chance at escape. Her limbs were sore from holding them up, but when she let them relax the ropes pinched into the skin she had made raw trying to break free earlier. She couldn't help it; she'd have to deal with the pain. When she rested her arms, her shoulders felt better.

Cori was restless. She drifted in and out of sleep. This time when she woke up, the man was sitting in one of her dining room chairs watching her sleep. The only light in the otherwise dark room was from the bathroom directly behind him. She was getting angry. She still couldn't tell who he was. The light was obscuring his features.

He rose from the chair slowly. Her breath froze in her lungs as he pulled something from his back pocket. She thought for sure this was it. He didn't come to her though. He went to her dresser first. She heard the distinct click of a lighter and relaxed some. He continued lighting candles

—that she had not purchased—all around the room. It would have been romantic if not for the madman who had her tied up.

The man turned to face her. Cori couldn't believe her eyes. "Luke? What are you doing here? Why are you doing this?"

"Did you really think you could take my wife away from me and not suffer any consequences?"

"I didn't take your wife, Luke. She killed herself." Cori kept her voice strong yet therapeutic. It was the voice she used with her patients. "Why don't you let me up and we can sit and discuss how you are feeling."

"I don't need to talk about my feelings."

"I'm sorry for your loss, but I was trying to help her."

He charged the bed, leaning over her angrily. "No. You confused her and manipulated her. She was mine and you wanted to take her from me." He screamed in her face. "Now, you can take her place."

"Her place?"

"You are gonna be mine. We're going to be together —forever."

That was the moment Cori realized she was never going to leave this room alive. Luke had beaten his wife almost daily, as well as mentally abused her. He was a narcissist and no amount of talking to him was going to help her...not that she was in a great position to calmly diagnose such things. *She* was the one in her underwear tied to her own bed.

He was looking at her as both a long-lost lover and predator eyeing his prey. Cori felt sick to her stomach. No matter what was wrong with him, his end game was the same regardless. Cori was living on borrowed time. Only Luke knew how much was left.

TANK

When Krysta parked in his driveway, he was surprised to see Cori's car wasn't in front of her house. She said she had a guy coming to put in a security system. It hadn't taken Paxton much more than a half hour to get here, and Cori left the party approximately fifteen minutes before he did. That was less than an hour. There's no way anyone could install an entire system in less than an hour.

Did she lie to him? No, he confirmed it with Mother. So where the hell was she? Krysta walked around to where he stood looking at the house.

"Where is she?"

"I don't know. I hoped maybe she had texted you. I guess not."

"No. She had an appointment thirty minutes ago. I'll call her and see where she is."

Krysta pulled her cell phone from her back pocket. Paxton waited impatiently as she held the phone to her ear. Soon, she lowered the phone to her side.

"No answer."

He scrubbed his hand across his face. "I have a bad feeling."

"Chill, we don't know anything. Maybe she canceled the appointment and went to the store."

"Then why didn't she answer your call?"

Krysta bit into her bottom lip. Worry was evident in her eyes. "I don't know."

At least he could count on her not to give him some bullshit lie. Krysta was always honest with him about important things. He jogged across the yard to Cori's door.

He tried the handle. Locked. He jogged around to the back door, but it was locked too. Maybe she really did go out.

Krysta was still standing in the driveway. She looked hopeful. He shook his head no. Her shoulders slumped. Paxton wrapped his arm around his sister's shoulders.

"Let's go inside and wait for her. Keep trying her phone too." He took one last look over at her house. "I'm gonna blister her ass when I see her."

Krysta giggled. "I really don't wanna hear about your fetishes. It's bad enough I had to see you two having sex." She scrunched her face up.

He laughed as they walked up the porch steps together. "That was your own damn fault."

Not knowing what else to do, and feeling pretty damn useless, he turned on the television and sat on the couch. Every few minutes he watched Cori's house from his window. Nothing out of the ordinary and no sight of his reckless neighbor.

Everyone she knew had been at the party, so she couldn't be with any of them. Unless she changed her mind and went back for him? Hope bubbled up inside of him and he called Gutter Mouth.

"Did you spank her?" he laughed into the phone instead of answering like a normal human being. Paxton felt his bubble of hope burst. Gutter Mouth wouldn't have asked him that if Cori was there.

"She's not home. No one is. Krysta and I are starting to get worried. Her car is gone. We hoped she had headed back there."

His friend's laughter died. "Sorry, man. I haven't seen her. You want me to come over?"

"Nah. She probably went shopping and we're overreacting. I'll call you later."

"Okay, I'm sure you're right. She'll turn up soon."

Paxton wasn't convinced. If he believed the sound of Gutter Mouth's voice, neither was he. This wasn't right. His gut was screaming at him.

Paxton woke up just before nightfall. He had fallen asleep in an awkward position and now his neck was stiff. He went to his window and looked over Cori's property. Her car was still missing. All the windows were dark. Where the fuck was she? Entering the kitchen, he found Krysta sitting at the breakfast table. She was watching Cori's house.

"Hey, you doing okay?"

Her eyes were red and he felt his heart break looking at her. "It's my fault if something happens to her."

He darted over to the table and wrapped her in his arms. She started crying again. He was completely helpless. He hadn't felt this way in a very long time. Not since the day his career with the BCPD ended. He smoothed her hair from her face, looking her in the eyes.

"This is *not* your fault. Don't even think that for one second."

She sobbed. "How can I not? I was looking after her. I let her leave without me."

"I should have been watching her. She was my responsibility and I fucked up because I let my dick do the thinking for me."

"I'm worried. It's been hours. I've called her every fifteen minutes, Paxton."

Every fifteen minutes for hours? *Shit.* "I am too."

Paxton rushed into the living room to grab his cell phone off of the table. He couldn't waste any more time sitting idle. He had to do something. He pulled up his contacts, found Mother's number, and hit the call button.

He answered after two rings. "What's up?"

"I think Cori is missing. I need your help, man."

There was a crash on the other end of the phone. Mother's voice sounded distant. "Shit," he yelled. Then everything sounded normal again. "Sorry, dropped the fucking phone. Tell me what happened."

"I haven't seen her since Max's place. She left to meet the installer and when I got to the house, her car wasn't here. It's been hours, man."

"Okay, don't stress. I'm running a trace on her phone and I'll put a BOLO out on her car. Hang on, let me call my guy at SafetyFirst."

Paxton could hear Mother talking on another phone. He walked over to the window. He watched for her car to pull up. *Willed* her fucking car to pull up. Every pair of headlights jolted his heart, only to be let down as the lights passed by.

Mother's voice brought his attention back. "Okay, now we can officially start to worry. The tech called in his arrival time, but never called in his departure. No one has heard from him since."

"Fuck!" Paxton bellowed. He began pacing the room like an agitated tiger. His muscles contracted as he flexed his fingers. He wanted to tear someone apart with his bare hands. If anyone fucking hurt Cori, they were done. Rage like he'd never felt roared inside of him.

Krysta ran into the room, her eyes wide with concern. "What? What happened?"

He held a hand up to silently tell her to hang on, as Mother continued to talk. "Her phone is pinging in her house. Wherever she is, her phone is home."

"Paxton," Krysta called to him from the window where she now stood.

He couldn't understand what Mother was saying. Why would her phone be home? She always seemed to carry it in her purse. If she was out shopping, she would have her purse.

Krysta yelled at him this time. "Paxton!"

"What? Damn it."

"Something isn't right."

"I know that, Krysta."

"No, asshole. Something at her house isn't right."

Paxton rushed to the window. Immediately he knew what she meant. Cori's car was still missing, but there was a soft glow flickering in an upstairs window. The glow became brighter. Paxton could tell it wasn't a light turning on. It was too soft and the light seemed to move. Candle glow? If she was home, where was her car? Why wasn't she answering her damn phone? Why the candles? He glanced at Krysta.

"Mother, call Foster. *Now*." He hung up the phone.

Krysta was silent for once. Tears still streaked down her face. He went to his end table and opened the drawer. Inside was a box with a combination lock. Punching in the code, the box unlocked. Inside was his Glock. He checked the magazine and chamber before tucking it into the back of his jeans.

Krysta approached him slowly. "Paxton, what are you doing?" She sounded terrified. She shouldn't be scared. Nothing would happen to her. He would make sure of that.

"I'm going over there. Mother is calling Foster. Call Kasper. He'll stay with you."

"Don't you want to wait for them?"

"If I wait, it could be too late. Stay here no matter what. Understand?"

"But I can help. Let me come with you."

"Absolutely not. Stay. Here."

He didn't have time to argue with her. He needed to find a way into the house undetected. Thanks to his brilliant job on the front door, it wouldn't be that way. The back door had a flip lock that could be a possibility.

He jogged around to the door. He took care to stay in the shadows close to the house. That way if anyone looked out, he wouldn't be easily seen.

He couldn't chance smashing the window pane. The noise would alert anyone inside to his presence. He grabbed a flathead screwdriver off the table next to Cori's gardening supplies. Gently, he wedged the screwdriver under the window pane closest to the lock. Careful not to shatter the pane of glass, he cracked the wood enough to slip the entire pane out of the window frame. He owed her another door. He hoped he wasn't too late to repay her.

He cursed at himself for thinking like that. Cori was going to be fine.

Reaching inside of the now glassless door frame, he quietly flipped the lock open. He prayed the door wouldn't creak as he guided it open enough to fit his body inside. He didn't bother shutting it behind him. The missing glass would snitch on him anyway.

Glock in hand, Paxton silently searched Cori's home for any sign of her or what might've happened to her. The kitchen and living room were empty. He noticed her purse on the floor, its contents scattered all over. Her cell phone included. Clenching his fist tighter around the grip of his gun, he continued toward the bottom of the stairs.

He could see a shadow dancing on the wall in the soft glow. Years on the force had taught him how to move his large body with stealth and agility. He ascended the stairs undetected.

The scene before him knocked the air right out of his lungs. He had to swallow down the urge to vomit. Cori was tied to the bed spread eagle with nothing on except her bra and panties. Tears streamed down her face. Some sick fuck sat naked kneeling between her thighs, stroking his cock.

Taking a step forward, Paxton was too focused on putting a bullet in the man's brain to see the laundry basket near the door. His leg brushed it, and it made a small scraping noise. The soon-to-be-dead man spun around, placing a steel blade against Cori's neck. *Fuck*. There went his element of surprise.

"Paxton?" Cori whispered to him.

"I'm here, sweetheart. Don't worry. Everything is going to be just fine."

The man shrieked at him. "Everything is not going to be fine! You're ruining everything."

"Luke. Luke. Look at me." Cori sounded so calm and collected, Paxton felt pride swell inside of himself. This woman was incredible.

This Luke character looked down at her. "Yes?"

"Everything will be fine. My friend is going to leave now and—"

"No! No one leaves." He pressed the knife into her neck harder. Paxton watched a bead of blood form under its tip. Could he get a shot off before he cut Cori's throat? "You, get over there where I can see you better. And drop the fucking gun."

Paxton took a step forward only to freeze when Luke remembered his gun. Without his weapon, he would have to disarm the guy. That would be much more difficult.

"I said lose the gun or I'll slice her throat right now. Throw it in the bathroom and shut the door."

Cori squeezed her eyes closed, fresh tears leaking from the corners. Defeated, Paxton put the safety back on and tossed the gun into the bathroom as he was told. He closed the door and waited.

Luke nodded his approval. "Good. Now sit in that chair. You can watch while I make Cori mine." His smile twisted Paxton's guts. Maybe if he put the knife down, he could rush him. One punch is all it would take to render the stupid fuck unconscious. He couldn't promise he'd stop there. In fact, he knew without a doubt that he would beat this man to death the first chance he got.

With his eyes glued to Paxton, the bastard began kissing Cori's face. Paxton clenched his jaw. He couldn't just fucking sit here and watch him violate her. What the hell could he do? He needed a distraction. Something to get this bastard's attention off of Cori. Maybe then he could disarm him. The man dragged the blade down toward her breasts.

"Don't," Paxton growled fiercely.

Luke pointed the knife at Paxton. "Don't tell me what to—"

He never finished his sentence. Instead the side of his head exploded. Paxton jumped up from where he had been ordered to sit. In the doorway stood Krysta. She was shaking horribly. The gun he had bought her was still pointed at the empty space where Luke's head had been. Cori's screams filled the room. Her face was splattered with his blood. His dead body drooped across hers.

Movement from behind Krysta demanded his attention. Gutter Mouth.

"Take care of Krysta," Paxton yelled. "I think she's in shock. I'll get Cori."

Sirens sounded in the distance. Paxton ran over to Cori. She was crying, but no longer screaming. He wouldn't have blamed her if she was. He rolled Luke's corpse off of her and tried to untie the ropes binding her. He could tell how hard she'd tried to get free over the hours she had been held captive. His gut turned thinking of what she must've felt up here alone with that sick fuck. She had pulled on the ropes so much, her wrists were raw and bloody. He didn't want to tug at them any more.

He looked around the room for something to use. There was nothing other than Luke's knife, but Paxton wasn't about to touch evidence. Not when it could potentially affect his little sister.

Paxton smoothed her hair from her face. "Hang on."

Leaping up from where he was on the bed, he hurried into the bathroom. Spotting his gun on the floor near the shower, he snatched it up and put it in his waistband. He opened the medicine cabinet and scrounged around. There was nothing helpful in there. Under the sink, however, he found a pair of scissors. He grabbed them and sat down on the edge of the bed closest to Cori's head. Her eyes were glazed over and she looked a million miles away.

Paxton clenched his jaw so tightly, it was painful. He glanced over at Krysta. She was hugging Gutter Mouth. The tears still shone on her cheeks. He wished he'd been the one to pull the trigger. He'd trained her to shoot in self-defense, but he'd never wanted his baby sister to live with the guilt of taking someone else's life. It wasn't something that ever left you.

He cut the rope that held up Cori's arms. He was careful to make sure he held on to them so they wouldn't drop like stones. He couldn't be certain how long they had been held up. He eased her arms down to the bed. Her moan of pain was heartbreaking.

He rose and moved to her feet. He cut both ropes holding her legs spread apart. She immediately closed them and curled her knees toward her chest. Both arms wrapped around her knees. She looked so fucking small as she lay there in a fetal position.

Foster came through the bedroom door with his gun drawn. "Everyone okay?"

Gutter Mouth nodded. "More or less."

Paxton continued to rub Cori's back, even though he wasn't sure she even registered anyone in the room. "Except Luke over there."

Foster looked confused. "Luke who?"

"I don't know. Cori called him by name. She's checked the fuck out right now though."

"I have an ambulance outside. They'll take care of her…Don't look at me like that, Tank. She needs to go, I need to talk to you. I need a statement."

"Fuck, Foster. Seriously? Now?"

"You should know the answer to that better than anyone."

Two paramedics maneuvered passed Gutter Mouth and Krysta. One of them Paxton had a brief encounter with last year. The other one he didn't know from Adam. The male paramedic stopped to talk to Krysta.

Shauna walked by, touching his arm. "Hey there, Tank." She smiled.

He ignored her in favor of eavesdropping on his sister. Not that he needed to be stealthy about it since Krysta began shouting for everyone to hear.

"I said I was fine, numb nuts. Now go help my friend,

or so help me God—"

Gutter Mouth rubbed her back. "Kitten. Pull your claws in. He's doing his job."

Krysta spun around to glare at him, only she never said a word. Unshed tears glistened in her eyes. She nodded and made her way to Cori's bedside. Knowing Krysta would be right there with Cori, Paxton knew now was a good time to talk to Foster.

Foster ushered him down the stairs and out the front door. They made it halfway into the yard when Foster turned to him.

"Okay, now tell me what happened."

Paxton took a deep breath and relayed what happened. He started with the moment he had noticed the flickering light in her upstairs window up until Krysta saved Cori from being raped and no doubt murdered before his eyes.

Foster's eyes widened. "Jesus. I'm so sorry, Tank."

"Yeah. Well, she's safe now."

"All right, I have everything I need. I'm sure a few other officers may question you after I put the report in since I'm closing the shooting as a self-defense, being as we're friends. I'll let Detective Martinez interview Krysta. I want someone else to take her statement so there's no ethical misconduct allegations."

"New guy?"

Foster nodded. "Yeah."

"You don't like him much, huh?"

Chuckling, Foster put his notebook into his back pocket. "How'd you know?"

Paxton smiled back. "You gave him my sister to question instead of me. Wasn't hard to figure out."

Krysta emerged from the house a second before the paramedics brought Cori out on the stretcher. He could see her wrists bandaged and her skin was ashen. Again, he had to tamp down his rage. Her eyes were closed. She looked almost peaceful, but in this case, he knew looks were definitely deceiving.

Paxton watched Detective Martinez take Krysta by the elbow. *Strike one, dude.* He walked over to the ambulance and covered Cori's hand with his.

"Cori?"

Her eyes fluttered open. She didn't say anything. She just squeezed his hand and closed her eyes again. Fresh tears leaked from their corners.

"Is she okay? Did he do something to her before I got there?"

He panicked thinking of what drugs that maniac could have given her before he arrived. He looked up at the paramedic with the name badge **'JONES.'**

"We gave her something to help her relax. Physically, she has some minor lacerations on her wrists and ankles. She suffered from a substantial amount of head trauma. That's where my concern is. Unfortunately, it's the doctor who will have to answer those questions and come up with a diagnosis. Emotionally and mentally, well, we can't say."

"Thank you."

Gutter Mouth stood next to him. "How's Doc?"

"I'm not sure, man."

Gutter Mouth patted him on the back. "She's a tough cookie. She's gonna be okay."

"I hope you're right. An ordeal like this...some people don't bounce back."

They were both silent until Gutter Mouth elbowed him in the ribs.

"What the—"

"Speaking of tough cookie." Gutter Mouth pointed to where Krysta stood. Now both hands were on her hips and she was blinking way too fast for the detective's own good. Paxton wanted to yell retreat, but he also wanted to watch the train wreck that was about to take place. The detective pointed his finger in her face. *Strike two, poor bastard.*

The paramedic, Jones, called over to him. "We're taking her to Mercy. If you want to follow us there."

"I will, thank you."

Krysta was running across the yard. "Don't you leave without me. I'm getting my phone. Shit, get hers so I can call her sister." She disappeared into his house.

He climbed Cori's front porch stairs. Foster stood there listening to Martinez relay his verbal report on the conversation with Krysta.

"Foster, I'm serious. I've never heard a woman talk like that in all my life. I don't even think everything she called me were real words...I think she literally made them up. Yet I still knew she was calling me something vulgar."

Foster laughed. "And yet you survived. Good job."

Paxton tried not to laugh. He went into the house. A CSU team was already hard at work dusting for prints. Paxton was bending over to pick up her phone when a voice startled him.

"You can't touch that," he scolded.

"I appreciate that, but I need to notify her sister."

The tech looked downright disgusted with him. "I understand. Now I need you to understand that I will not have my crime scene tainted by a civilian with no sense."

"I'm gonna shove my sense up your ass, you—"

"Tank," Foster yelled from the doorway. "I don't need

any more paperwork. I'll notify her sister. I have her information back at the station. Leave my techs alone."

Paxton purposely growled at the tech before turning his back on him. His sister was waiting in his truck for him. He trotted over and climbed into the driver's seat. He pulled out of the driveway and drove as fast as he dared to Mercy Hospital.

He stole a glance at her. "How are you holding up? The truth. No bullshit between us."

"I don't think it's really hit me yet. So for now, I really am okay. However, I don't think I can be alone for a little while. So if you don't mind your little sister cramping your style a while longer, I'd like to stay with you."

He took one hand off the wheel and squeezed hers. "You're my kid sister. I love you. You're always welcome to stay with me. If you need to talk to someone, I know some great counselors. They've helped a lot of guys on the force."

"Thank you."

They finished the ride to the hospital in silence, both of them lost in their own thoughts. After three laps through the parking lot, a space finally opened up. Krysta was out of the truck before he pulled the key from the ignition. He followed her inside, where they were told they weren't family and would have to sit and wait.

Paxton thought about telling them he was her fiancé since it worked so well for Max back when Sloane had been admitted. But since he was an asshole who'd fucked two of the nurses just last month, he didn't think anyone would buy it. Even if they did, he didn't want anyone to think he'd been cheating on Cori with them. So he took a seat and waited. And waited. And waited.

Krysta stood up abruptly. "Brianna?"

The woman came over to where they sat. He could tell she had been crying—her makeup was smudged and her nose was red. She was taller than Cori, but they shared the same facial features. Where Cori's hair was long and black, this woman's was short and more of a dark burgundy.

"Krysta?"

The women hugged each other like they were long-lost friends. He felt incredibly out of the loop. Luckily, Gutter Mouth came bounding in with Max and Sloane on his heels. Sloane beelined to where the women stood embracing. Max and Gutter Mouth came to stand with him.

Max looked over at the nurse's station. "Anything?"

"No, bastards wouldn't tell me anything because I'm not family."

They sat down in the hard-ass plastic chairs to wait some more. The women bombarded the nurse's station. It couldn't have been more than five minutes before a doctor was quietly talking to them. Cori's sister, Brianna, threw her arms around Krysta. She buried her head in his sister's shoulder. Dread settled in his stomach. He couldn't sit and wait anymore. Paxton jumped up from his seat.

"What's going on?" he demanded.

No one answered. Krysta was comforting Brianna and Sloane was still talking to the doctor. *Okay, this is bullshit.* Couldn't they see he was worried too? She was his responsibility. She got hurt on his watch. Someone had better give him some fucking answers.

He bellowed, "I *said* what the fuck is going on?"

Sloane glared at him. "Tank, go sit the hell down."

Feeling like a scolded child, he resumed his seat between Max and Gutter Mouth. Paxton looked over at Max.

"Dude, your woman yelled at me."

"Yeah...well." Max shrugged his shoulders.

Gutter Mouth snorted. "Did you leave your balls at home? I'll go get some answers."

He got up and started toward the girls. Sloane must have sensed him coming. She turned around and gave him a look that Paxton could only describe as haunting. Gutter Mouth immediately turned around and took his seat.

Max smiled. "You were saying?"

"No shit, I think my balls just shriveled up. Your woman scared my balls. Not cool, bro."

The doctor left, disappearing behind a locked door. Sloane whispered in the girls' ears and walked toward them. Gutter Mouth cupped his balls while whispering sweet things to them until she stopped in front of them.

"Okay, now that I know what's going on, I can relay it to you." She gave all of them a pointed look. "Cori suffered some head trauma. She has a fractured skull. It's not as severe as they originally thought, but it's enough that she needs to stay here under observation. There doesn't seem to be any hemorrhaging. So that's a really good sign."

"How? How did she get her head fractured tied to the bed, Sloane?" he asked through clenched teeth.

"They believe she was subdued by having her head strike the floor hours before you found her." He could feel his blood pressure rising rapidly. "Tank, calm down. She's going to be fine."

"That fucker is lucky he's dead. I need some air." He got up and stormed outside.

He walked around the building until he found a secluded area where he knew no one would easily spot him. Anger boiled inside of him. He pulled back and punched the dumpster he stood next to. A large dent indicated his rage.

He leaned against the brick building, sliding down so he was hunched in the grass. He lowered his face into his hands. He was overwhelmed with emotion. She could have died. He felt the wet warmth of tears on his palm. He lifted his head and stared at his hands. He was crying? He hadn't shed a tear when he left the police force. He hadn't even cried when things ended with Gillian.

He didn't know how to navigate these feelings. How was he going to go back in there and face her?

TWELVE
CORI

CORI WOKE up in a hospital room alone. Where was everyone? Where was Paxton? Her heart sank a little. She could feel a bandage around her head as well as her arms and legs. Her head felt like it was in a vise. The pounding seemed like it was beating in time to the rhythm of her heart.

She wanted to vomit. Bolting upright, she grabbed the bucket on the rolling tray next to the bed and dry heaved.

She didn't think she was ever going to stop. Now in addition to her head, her stomach and throat hurt. She pressed the call buzzer. Almost immediately a nurse came in.

"How are you doing, honey?" the short, silver-haired nurse asked her.

Cori's voice sounded gravelly even to her own ears. "Water, please."

"Oh sure thing. I'll be right back."

The nurse disappeared just as quickly as she had entered. Cori lay back on her pillow. The lights were dimmed, but still they seemed too bright. She tried to recall what happened, but she couldn't remember everything. Paxton had come for her after all. He must have shot Luke. No…Paxton couldn't have been the one to shoot him. She'd been looking right at Paxton. It wasn't until she had felt the spray of warm blood on her face that she'd closed her eyes. So who shot him?

The nurse came back in with a Styrofoam cup filled with ice and water. "Sip at it, dear. Don't guzzle."

A doctor entered reading her chart. "Dr. Transue. How are you feeling?"

"I have the worst headache I've ever experienced in my entire life."

"Well, you had some head trauma that resulted in a slight skull fracture and a concussion. So a headache is completely normal. So is nausea, vomiting, dizziness, loss of balance, and a few other things we will watch out for. I'll have the nurse bring you something to dull the pain. Luckily, your other injuries were much less severe."

Cori could attest to some of those symptoms already. The doctor continued.

"Your ankles had minor scratches. Your wrists, however, suffered a little more damage. Nothing that won't heal on its own over time. I do recommend that you put some Neosporin or something like it on the wounds to help heal them with minimal scarring. Also, take it easy for a while. No activity that could have you reinjured. No bike riding of any kind for a few months. Be smart when exercising. First and foremost, rest. For no less than two weeks. Think couch potato." He smiled warmly at her.

"I understand, doctor."

"Good. Now, if you're feeling up to it, there is a small crowd in the waiting room wondering how you are. Shall I have them come back or would you rather rest? For the record, I prefer you rest."

"Can I see them, please?"

"I figured you'd say that. Only for a few minutes."

"Thank you."

Once the doctor was gone, Cori scooted herself up in the bed some. She didn't want to look pathetic when Paxton came in. She fixed the sheets around her, smoothing them in place, and rested her hands on top. It didn't take long before her door opened. Krysta came barreling in first. Cori was being squeezed to death as everyone else entered the room. Gutter Mouth closed the door behind him with a sad look on his face. The one person missing was Paxton. The door opened again and excitement flooded through her. Paxton?

"Bri."

Brianna hurried to her and wrapped her arms around her shoulders. "You scared me. Don't do that again."

"I'm sorry."

Cori felt a tear slip from her eye. Brianna was crying freely. She missed her sister. With everything that had happened, maybe she should go stay with her for a while after all? Her house held so many bad memories now. How could she go back there?

As if she'd read her mind, Brianna smiled sadly at her. "You can come stay with me. For as long as you want."

"Thank you."

Krysta sat on the edge of the bed, hurt evident on her beautiful face. "What about us?"

Brianna looked confused. "I don't understand?"

"Why don't you stay with me and Paxton?"

Cori whispered as if everyone in the room couldn't hear her anyway. "I can't do that."

"Why not?"

The door opened again and this time Paxton entered the room. "Hey, Doc." He smiled, but it didn't reach his eyes. Something wasn't right. His knuckles looked red and now that she was really looking, so did his eyes. He noticed her looking at his hands again and shoved them into his pockets.

Krysta took ahold of her hand. "We care about you too. None of us want to see you go."

It wasn't long before Sloane interrupted the conversation. "Sweetie, I'm really sorry. We have to run. Mother has been watching Mia and we need to get home."

"Please don't apologize. I'm grateful that you both came by."

"Of course we would be. You're one of us." She winked before walking over to the door to where Max stood. He waved goodbye to Cori and they left.

Brianna stood up. She stretched her arms above her head. "I'm going to grab a soda. Does anyone want anything?"

They all declined and Brianna left the room. It only took ten seconds before Krysta started in. She looked around the room at everyone. "She wants to leave us."

Cori smiled sadly. "Krysta, you don't even live around here."

"Yeah, but I'm in town often enough."

Paxton's gaze met his sister's. "What are you talking about?"

"She's thinking of moving in with Brianna."

Cori waited for Paxton to tell her to stay. She waited for him to offer his home to her like he did before. He came for her tonight. That must've meant something. She waited.

"If that's what she really wants to do, Krysta, we can't make her stay."

Cori thought she might actually be feeling her heart breaking. It took superhuman strength to hold back the tears.

Gutter Mouth placed his hand on Krysta's shoulder. "You look tired, Doc." He knew somehow that she was barely hanging on. She could tell by the sadness reflected in his own eyes. "Let's let her get some sleep, kitten."

Krysta leaned down to hug her. "Please, think about it."

"I will," she lied.

Paxton maneuvered himself to her bedside. Leaning down, he kissed her forehead. "Get some rest. We'll see you soon."

Cori watched as they left her hospital room. She couldn't hold the tears back any longer. She had a feeling that she had just said goodbye to Paxton for good.

———

TANK

"You're a selfish, no good bastard of a chicken shit," Krysta screamed at him at the top of her lungs after an intensely quiet elevator ride.

He waited until they were out of the waiting room and in the parking lot to answer her. "What the fuck did I do this time?"

"You don't know?" she screeched. She turned to Gutter Mouth. "He really doesn't know?"

"No, Krysta, I really don't know," Paxton snarled back at her.

She stopped in her tracks. She whispered almost too softly for him to hear her, "She wanted you to ask her to stay."

Was that true? Did she still want him after he'd failed her? There was no way. Only...maybe she did. Could he take that chance? What if she needed him and he fucked up again? No. He couldn't risk her again. He fucked up. He broke his promise to protect her. She was better off far away from him.

"I'm not good enough for her, Krysta. She needs to find someone better."

"Paxton..."

"Please, can we drop it?"

He wasn't sure if it was the look in his eyes or the sound of his voice, but for the first time ever, his baby sister didn't argue with him.

Paxton glanced at Gutter Mouth once they started walking again. "Are you coming to the house?"

"Nah. I'm gonna head home and get some sleep. I'll talk to you in the morning."

"All right."

They bumped fists and Paxton climbed into his truck. Krysta was already inside staring out of the passenger window. It was dark. He didn't know what she could be looking at. He couldn't see anything other than parked cars. But maybe her mind was replaying this evening. God knows his was. His knuckles still hurt from punching the dumpster out back, but not as bad as his pride.

He couldn't forgive himself. He'd been too worried about getting her out of his damn head to focus on his job. Lack of focus got people hurt. He knew that. He needed to refocus himself. The only way he knew how was by letting her go.

———

It had been three weeks since he'd seen Cori. He'd never returned to the hospital and he had been on a job the day she'd moved out. He regretted not being there to say goodbye to her. At the same time, he was relieved not to have had to watch her go. She still haunted his dreams every night. He saw her lying in her bed. Sometimes he made it in time to save her, sometimes he didn't. Those were the nights he woke up covered in sweat, ready to break her door down. Then reality would sink in. She didn't need him because she wasn't there.

Krysta talked to her almost every day. Usually whispers that stopped once he entered the room. Today was no different. She was sitting at the kitchen table on her laptop working with her earbuds in so she could talk hands free.

"Oh hey, let me call you back."

She hung up the phone and went back to her work. He crossed his arms over his chest and stared at her until she looked up.

"What?"

"Was that Cori?"

She glared at him. "As a matter of fact, it was."

"How is she?"

"None of your damn business."

He was instantly pissed off. Hell, he was pissed off a lot lately. "What the fuck do mean, none of my business?"

She looked at him like he was a piece of shit. "I mean, if you cared so fucking much, you'd call her yourself. Prick."

She packed up her things and stormed out of the room. He plopped himself in the nearest chair. She was right, of course. That's exactly what he should do. He shouldn't have had let her go in the first place. He had fucked up, but that's because he'd been fighting his feelings. He pounded his fist on the table, disgusted with himself. Krysta was right. He was a chicken shit.

With his mind made up, Paxton ran back upstairs to shower and get dressed.

He wasn't going to call her. *Fuck that.* She was his girl. He was going to go get her. He grabbed a pair of blue jeans, a black cotton t-shirt, and his Fear Incorporated ball cap. He was walking out of the house when his past got out of her car.

Gillian smiled at him. He braced himself for the feeling she had always stirred in him. Only this time, there was nothing. She didn't look like his dream girl. She looked like a nightmare. He thought back to the good times they'd had. He had to admit, before he knew Gillian was cheating on him, they'd been happy. She had treated him good. That's when he realized why he'd been holding back with Cori: He was afraid he wouldn't know if it happened again. But Cori wasn't Gillian.

He couldn't tell the future. But he *did* know the future would be bleak without taking a chance with Cori. And just like that, his anger toward Gillian was gone.

Gillian had given him the opportunity to find Cori.

"What could you possibly want from me, Gill?"

She smoothed down her extremely tight skirt. "I made a mistake. I'm here to make things work with us. I was stupid. I'm sorry."

This is a joke, right? Paxton laughed loudly. No, he didn't just laugh—he held his mid-section and belly laughed until Krysta came outside to find out what was going on. Gillian had confusion written all over her face, which only added gasoline to the fire.

"What the fuck is she doing here?" Krysta yelled with

her hands fisted at her sides. "I swear on our parents, may they rest in peace. Paxton, if you even entertain the thought, I will kick both of your asses here and now."

He held up a hand to Krysta. "Give me some credit." He turned toward his ex. "Gillian, you're barking up the wrong tree. Once upon a time we could've been great, but not now. Or ever. Thanks for the laugh, but I have to go pick up my girlfriend now."

Gillian didn't try to hide the surprise on her face. "Girlfriend?"

Krysta jumped up with her fist in the air. "Hell yes. Let me grab my phone."

He watched her run inside. "Wait, what?" Now he was the one that was confused.

Gutter Mouth picked that moment to pull up on his Harley. He lifted his helmet off and glared at Gillian. "What the hell did I miss, dude?"

Krysta stormed out of the house like a woman on a mission, slamming his front door behind her hard enough to rattle the windows. "We're going to get Cori." She beamed.

Gutter Mouth shut off his engine. "Count me in."

"Shot gun!" Krysta teased and ran for the front passenger door. She made it a moment before Gutter Mouth and being the brat she was, she stuck her tongue out at him before hopping inside. "I win."

"This time, kitten." He grinned.

What the hell was going on? Deciding it was best to just go with the flow for once, he hurried to his truck. He'd just opened the door when he remembered Gillian was still standing there, dumbstruck.

"We gotta go. It's over. Don't come back here." He got

in, closing the door. "By the way," he called. "That lipstick looks whorish. I'd rethink that color."

And off they went.

It seemed as though he had been driving for days when in reality it had only been a couple of hours. Since Krysta had Brianna's address, he was able to show up unannounced and uninvited. All women loved that. *Yeah, right.* He pulled up to a small white ranch-style house. The front lawn was manicured nicely. Flowery bushes lined the front under the windows. He wondered if Cori had a hand in its conception.

Her car was sitting in the driveway. He suddenly felt nervous. No, he wasn't going to chicken out. He was going to do this.

"You two wait here."

Krysta pouted. "Aww, come on. I wanna watch you grovel. Ass face here does too."

Paxton smiled at her. "Abso-fuckin-lutely not."

"At least we can see if she slaps the shit outta him," Gutter Mouth chimed in.

Krysta shrugged. "True."

Paxton took a deep breath and got out of his truck. He should have stopped for flowers, but between his nerves and the two adult children he'd had bickering the whole ride, he'd completely forgot. He knocked on the front door. Maybe he should have called instead. Maybe he should have—

His mind went blank as Cori opened the door. *Fuck.* She was beautiful. She just stood there, staring at him.

Say something, he mentally scolded himself. Only he didn't know what to say. *I'm an asshole, please forgive me?* "Hello," he blurted.

"What are you doing here?" She looked around him to

where his truck sat. Gutter Mouth and Krysta had their faces in the window and Krysta was smiling and waving like a happy circus monkey. Why did he bring them? Oh, that's right, they didn't give him a choice.

"I came for you." He held up his hand to silence whatever it was she had been about to say. "Let me say this, please."

She nodded her head. He couldn't read her expression at all. It was now or never and his gut told him not to lose this woman. Swallowing his pride, he hoped what he had to say would be enough.

"I'm sorry. I should have never let you walk away. I was scared. I didn't think I was good enough for you. I still don't, but I'm a selfish bastard and I want you anyway. I know I hurt you, but if you give me a chance, I'll make it up to you. I think there's something here worth fighting for. I think you feel it too. Please, Cori. I've missed the fuck out of you. Come home."

———

CORI

She couldn't believe Paxton was standing in front of her, much less saying that he had missed her. She had so many emotions running through her that she couldn't hold them back any longer. Tears streamed down her face. Concern and uncertainty showed clearly on his. She smiled at him. This beast of a man that she was crazy about was here and he wanted to be with her. She opened the screen door and threw her arms around him.

"Paxton," she whispered.

Krysta and Gutter Mouth catcalled from his truck and they both laughed.

He squeezed her tighter. "Did I have you at hello?"

She looked up at him. "Not even close."

He smirked. "No?"

"You came for me. You took your sweet ass time, but you came for me."

"Come home with me, Cori."

"I want to, but…" She lowered her head in defeat. "I just can't stay in that house. Not yet."

He slipped his calloused fingers under her chin, lifting her head. "Who said anything about you staying in that house?"

"I don't understand?" She didn't dare say what she had hoped he meant.

He cupped her face in both of his hands and looked into her eyes. "I said, come home with me. I want you in *my* house. No, make that *our* house. In our bed, because, sweetheart, I have a whole lot of making up to do to you."

His grin ignited everything inside of her. She wanted him to start right this very minute. Unfortunately, Krysta and Gutter Mouth were still watching intently from the truck.

"So should I go get my things now or send for them later?" She giggled.

"You won't be needing anything except my shirt for a few days. Leave it all."

Paxton slipped an arm under her butt and threw her over his shoulder in a fireman's carry. Swinging her around, he started marching toward his truck.

"Paxton," she screamed through her laughter. "I need my purse and my phone." He continued to walk like a man on a mission. "Paxton, I need to lock the door."

Paxton opened the truck door and placed her inside. He swung her legs in and shut the door. He turned to Gutter Mouth and Krysta, who were both in the back seat now. "Don't let her go anywhere." He winked at her before turning back to the house.

A few minutes later, he emerged with her purse in one hand and her phone in the other. He raised them both in the air like prizes while he jogged back to her. He handed them over through the open window.

"Thank you."

He grinned like a kid before rounding the truck to get in. Once inside, he leaned over, slipping his hand behind her neck. She felt her pulse quicken before his lips even touched hers. He pulled her forward and claimed her lips. His kiss was intense and thorough. It took her breath away.

Krysta leaned over the front seat. "Okay, can we just get home now?"

"Yeah, yeah," Paxton responded. He started the truck and headed for the highway. Paxton took her hand, lifted it to his lips, and placed a soft kiss on her knuckles. Without letting her hand go, he veered onto the highway headed home.

EPILOGUE

TANK

HOW LONG DOES it take for one woman to get ready? He'd been pacing around like an expectant father for twenty minutes.

He stopped at the bottom of the stairs and yelled, "Woman, what is taking you so long?"

"Don't rush me, Tank. I want to look nice."

"You'd look beautiful in a burlap sack. Now hurry the hell up."

"Did you get the gift from on our bed?" she called after him.

Shit. He almost forgot. "Of course I didn't." He took the steps two at a time. The colorfully wrapped gift sat on the bed. He looked around. Cori had the bathroom door closed. He figured he might as well go sit down. He picked up the present and movement caught his eye.

Cori stood in the bathroom doorway in a white sundress. Her hair fell in waves over her shoulders. The dress ended just above her knees, showing off a great pair of tanned legs. He thought he might have to pick his jaw up off the floor before they could leave. She walked into the closet. She came back out with a pair of white strappy heeled shoes. He had no idea what they were actually called.

"No way. You need to change." She looked at him like he had grown a second head and horns. He chuckled. "I'm serious. I'll wait."

"What's wrong with what I'm wearing?"

"I'll have to kill someone if you go out like that."

Realization flashed across her face. Her face softened. "Thank you, but I'm not changing. You won't be killing anyone either. It's Mia's birthday."

She was right, of course. He would just have to stay close by and give anyone who looked at Cori a death stare. He couldn't believe sweet little Mia was a year old already. He remembered the day she was born like it was yesterday. She was so tiny; he was afraid to hold her. Sloane insisted. She had told him it was important that Mia know him from the start. She had said Mia needed to know there were good men that she could trust in her life.

He'd held that tiny angel in his arms that day. He'd promised her he would always watch out for her and protect her. She had been the one thing that mattered to him. Until now. Cori stopped in front of him.

She put her hand over his heart. "Is everything okay?"

He smiled. "How could it not? I get to spend the day with my two best girls."

"You do understand that the only girl I will share you with is that sweet baby. Don't you?"

"Do you really think I'm that stupid?" She opened her mouth to speak. Before she could, he took her lips in a searing kiss. When he pulled away, he winked. "Please don't answer that."

They arrived at Max's house just minutes before Gutter Mouth. Everyone else was already there. Krysta was in the kitchen with Bella and Sloane. Krysta had gone back home a week after Cori returned to them. She said she couldn't keep avoiding her life. He was glad she made it to the party. Paxton kissed Cori's cheek.

"Have fun." He swatted her ass before leaving her to find the guys.

They were in the living room with the kids. He was surprised they could sleep through all the noise. Max and Foster were discussing Bella's pregnancy. Gutter Mouth and Mother were talking about going to the Harley store next weekend for some big annual sale. In a chair near the corner watching the children was a man Paxton hadn't seen in over a year.

Benji stood up once he noticed him. "Holy shit, brother. How the fuck have you been?"

Benji ran his fingers through his long hair. His hair had always been on the short side, so it was weird to see it to his shoulders. He had a full beard too. He looked great, if not tired. Not the kind of tired that a weekend of sleep could cure. He looked like his *soul* was tired. Paxton had nothing but respect for the man.

"I've been busy." He looked at the kids sleeping in the playpen. "Dude, I've missed so much. I hear you even settled down." He snorted.

"Yeah, she's great." Paxton smiled just thinking of her. His gut twisted at the expression on Benji's face. "You didn't come here for a social visit, did you?"

"I wish it was only social. I've missed you guys and

I'm glad I could make it, but I do have news too. I wanted to wait until you were all here."

The conversation in the room stopped as if someone had pulled a plug. It was an eerie quiet. The sound of the girls' laughter carried in from the kitchen. They all shared a look. Whatever Benji had to say, should they be included?

Max took the lead on the situation. "I think this should stay between us for now."

Agreement echoed throughout the room. Benji nodded his understanding.

"Lupis Petrov died yesterday morning."

Max covered his face with his hands. "Fuck," he spat.

Paxton thought that would be a good thing, but obviously he had missed a memo somewhere.

Gutter Mouth was the first to chime in. "So? Ivan Petrov is nothing like his old man. As soon as he surfaces, we take him down and Sloane testifies it was him and Booker that killed Detlef."

Max paced the room. "Sloane was right when she said Detlef had his fingers in a lot of pies. Too bad not all of them were legal. There's no such thing as dissolving a partnership with people like that."

Paxton looked to Benji. "So her testimony would be the end of it?"

Mother stood up from the couch. "It's not that easy. Ivan has been in hiding for that reason. With his father dead, he *has* to show his face. He's about to take over the family business. He's not going to do that until he knows Sloane is neutralized."

Benji looked at Max. "Taking out Detlef wasn't a part of the old man's plan. He needed him alive. So, Ivan cost his father a lot of coin. The type of coin a man like that would kill over."

Gutter Mouth whistled. "Wow, even his own kid?"

Benji shrugged his shoulders. "I heard from a close informant, as long as Ivan stayed gone, there would be no problem with the old man. That's why Sloane has been safe up until now."

Shit had just gone from bad to worse. He knew it and every guy in the room knew it too. With Lupis dead, there was no one standing between Sloane and a bullet. Except them. The women's laughter grew louder as they approached.

Max rubbed the stubble on his face. "Okay, we'll come up with a plan later."

Sloane eyed Max suspiciously. "What are you guys being all secretive about?"

He smiled slyly at her. "I'm trying to convince them to hold a surprise wedding since my love won't make up her mind on a date yet."

"Don't you dare, Maxwell Fear," she warned tenderly.

She embraced him and the conversation once again took on an easy feeling. Cori came to stand next to Paxton.

"Is everything all right?" she asked.

"Yeah, why?"

"Just a feeling."

"Look around you, Doc. I have my best friends and the woman I'm crazy about here with me. It can't get much better than this."

She smiled up at him. "You're crazy about me?"

"Damn right I am."

"You better be." She winked.

Paxton wrapped his arms around her. He gazed around the room. Gutter Mouth and Krysta were butting heads again. Max and Slone were talking with Bella and Foster, while Mother and Benji peered down at the next generation still sleeping in the playpen. He knew they would have to do something about the Petrov situation, but for now, he couldn't remember the last time he had felt this happy or carefree. He looked forward to each day now. He looked forward to spending them with the amazing woman currently in his arms.

The End

BEFORE YOU GO...

If you enjoyed my book please take a quick second to leave a short review on Amazon. These reviews help me as an author be found by other amazing readers like you.

Thank you so much! :)

Keep reading for a *sneak peek* at Fear Inc: Volume 3.

SNEAK PEEK

FEAR INC: VOLUME 3

FEAR INC: VOLUME 3

PROLOGUE

Six Years Ago

Krysta rolled over onto her side, resting her head on her perched hand, to get a better view of Kasper as he stood by the cliff's edge overlooking their little town. He was gorgeous. The moonlight caressed his bare shoulders and back from this angle. The soft breeze tousled his hair. It was longer than it was when they started seeing each other six months ago. Now it would actually stay behind his ear and curl around the lobe when he pushed it there.

She never tired of looking at him. She knew if he'd asked her, she would gladly look her fill for the rest of her life. She sat up, rummaging around their blankets for her clothes. She stood up, slipping her feet into her panties before pulling her jeans on. Once her bra and shirt were back on, she wrapped her arms around him from behind. He crossed his arms around hers, holding her to him.

"Hey there, Kitten. It's getting late. As much as I don't want to, I better get you home."

He turned to face her, a big goofy smile on his lips.

Krysta stretched up on her tip-toes, pressing a kiss to them. It was soft and sweet. Nothing like the heated wet kisses of earlier, yet no less mesmerizing.

"You're so unbelievably beautiful." He pressed his lips to hers again.

Kissing Kasper had been a fantasy for longer than she cared to admit even to herself. Now, she could indulge whenever her heart desired. Well, not really, they were still hiding their relationship from everyone. That was why she needed to woman up. They wouldn't be able to hide much longer. She'd been nervous all night. She had to tell him. This moment. In their place, was perfect.

"Before we go, I have something to tell you."

"You can tell me anything." He grinned down at her, clasping his hands at the small of her back. "What dirty little fantasy are you cooking up now?"

I wouldn't call it a dirty fantasy. Perhaps scandalous. She sucked in a large breath, slowly blowing it out.

"I'm pregnant." She smiled up at him. There she said it. Now it suddenly felt real. As if sharing the news with him made it real and not just a notion. She had loved Kasper for so long, even though she wasn't ready now, she would get there. She had seven months to prepare. There wasn't anyone else she would want to do this with. Kasper was it for her. She knew it like she knew her own name.

The smile she so dearly loved slowly slipped from his face. "Are you playin' with me?"

"Of course not. Who would do such a thing?"

"You're pregnant?"

"Yes." She couldn't understand why he was looking at her that way.

He let go of her and took a step back. "Is it mine?"

"Is it…" She felt as though he'd smacked her in the

face. It would have hurt a lot less if he had. "You're the only one I've ever been with, and you fucking know it, Kass."

He ran his fingers through his hair, refusing to make eye contact. She touched his arm, only to have him pull away. She understood it was probably a shock. Hell, it was to her too when she found out. When the package says ninety-nine percent effective, you never think you'll be the one percent. Lucky her. Kasper pulled his shirt back on, then picked up their blanket.

"Kasper, talk to me," she pleaded.

"If we don't leave now, you'll miss curfew."

He left her standing there alone as he started down the footpath. Krysta could either follow or get left out here. She scurried after him. She could hear his Harley roar to life before she even cleared the tree line. His head was lowered as he held out her helmet. She slipped it on her head before swinging her leg over the bike. At least he waited for her to wrap her arms around him before he took off. The ride back to town was tense. He didn't squeeze her hands or reach back to rub her thigh while her drove like he usually did.

Krysta couldn't help the sinking feeling in her stomach. The one saying this was the last ride she would take with her arms wrapped around the man she desperately loved. Kasper stopped his bike at the end of her street like always. Kasper thought it would be better to see how things went before they broke the news to Paxton. He didn't want to lose his best friend and Krysta didn't want her brother to worry if it ended up being just a fling.

For her, it wasn't a fling. Every molecule of her being was madly in love with Kasper Guttenmuth.

She couldn't bring herself to get off the bike. Now that

she thought about it, it would be the last time she'd ride behind him, holding him tight. No matter what happened between them, it wasn't safe for her. She couldn't risk anything happening to the baby now. He felt stiff under her arms, his hands remaining on the handlebars. Slowly she dismounted.

"Kasper," she whispered.

"I'm sorry I said that. I know you haven't been with anyone else."

Relief flooded through her. Maybe he just needed some time. It took her a whole week to tell him.

"Don't worry. I'll pay for it," he said while tucking her helmet into his saddlebag.

"Pay for what?"

"The abortion. It's my responsibility."

For the second time tonight Krysta felt her world tip. Abortion. How could he even suggest that? She'd mentioned a few times, in the last six months alone, her feelings on that topic. She was pro-choice, but her choice was no. She would rather raise this baby on her own. She really hoped she wouldn't have to.

She straightened her shoulders, holding her head high. "I'm not doing that. I'm having this baby."

"Damn it, Krysta. This wasn't supposed to happen."

"Maybe we didn't plan it, but it did happen."

"I'm not the fathering type."

"Obviously, you are."

"I can't be someone's father, Krysta. Not now, maybe not ever."

Krysta felt her heart splintering into a million pieces. She pressed her shaking hands to her stomach as nausea rolled through her. She wasn't sure if it was from the realization she was going to be raising this baby on her own after all, or if morning sickness was once again rearing its ugly head. Unable to breathe through it, she turned quickly to the hedges behind her to vomit.

"Are you gonna be okay to walk home?"

The burning in her throat lit a fuse to ignite a fire in her belly. He didn't get to see her vulnerable ever again. Her father's words echoed in her ear. *"A man worthy of your love, baby girl, will always show you what you mean to him. Don't listen for flowery words. He may not know how to speak to them, but he will always show you if you're paying attention."*

Straightening, she wiped her mouth on the sleeve of her sweatshirt. Kasper still straddled his bike. She'd hoped she would see regret or pain in his eyes. Something to show her what he felt for her. Nothing. That's what she saw looking back at her. A blank mask devoid of any emotion, good, bad, or indifferent. This was it. It was time for her to walk away. Time to go back to pretending she wasn't in love with the man before her. She'd had to do just that for years. She could do it again. Fake it till you make it, they say.

"You don't need to worry about me anymore, Kasper." Without waiting for him to reply, she started walking down the dark street to her house. Alone.

ACKNOWLEDGMENTS

I want to take a moment to thank Limitless Publishing for believing in Fear Inc. Lori, you're always there to answer any question, big or small. I'd be lost without you. Sydnee, I'm so happy to be working closely with you on this project. You smooth out the edges and help me to be a better writer. There are countless authors that I've met along the way that have inspired and cheered me on. There are just too many of you to list, but know I adore you all.

My readers, without you I wouldn't be here. I hope you enjoy spending some of your precious time in my world as much as I enjoyed creating it.

RJ, for believing in me even when I found it hard to believe in myself.

Last, but certainly not least, my three amazing children: Taylor, Madison, and Aidan. Thank you for understanding deadlines, quiet time, and pizza night. No matter what I do, you three will always be my greatest accomplishment. I love you.

ABOUT THE AUTHOR

Melinda Valentine was born in upstate New York. Being the youngest of four children (and the only girl) made it easy for her to turn to books as companions. As a young child, she was whisked away to Baltimore, Maryland and spent her youth reading books such as *Nancy Drew*, *The Chronicles of Narnia*, and *The Little House on the Prairie* saga.

However, it wasn't until she was twelve years old that she read a book (Stephen King's *IT*) that made her realize that someday, she would herself become a writer. After that, her first (horrible) manuscript came to life, and at thirteen she had received her very first rejection letter. Heartbroken, she continued to read even more to learn about the craft of writing.

Today Melinda calls West Virginia home, with her swoon-worthy husband, hilarious children, and three crazy puppies of all ages. She hopes her readers fall in love with her characters as much as she has.

Website:
http://www.melindavalentine.com/